Scars of a Butterfly
(Urban Street Literature by: A.Dakala)

Synopsis: Dudley Keys was a street smart brother

who was hard on the outside, but soft on the inside.

To accomplish his goals as a computer analyst and

one day owning his own chain of barbershops,

Dudley knew he had to make a few life changes.

His live in girlfriend, Porsche Randals, was a hood

chick out to find the next big baller to get her to the

next level in her life. She often made poor

decisions, frequently lied and has known to cheat on

her boyfriends when not given enough attention.

Dudley at times didn't make good decisions

himself, Porsche knew exactly how to get to

Dudley, just offer him some anytime sex. In the

back of Dudley's mind, he knew she sometimes

were a road block for him to reach success. A

1

relationship well over due for a break up, Dudley accepted a job further south of the city where he was born and raised. His new lifestyle had plenty of adjustments, by landing a job nearly three hours away, from the crime riddled city of Baltimore, Maryland didn't make things that much easier, since he was leaving behind his girlfriend of 2 years only during the weekdays, and a hand full of homeboys he's known since childhood. Little did he know that a female co-worker (Troyia Patterson) he just met would not only make choices difficult, but she who would change his thoughts, his life and relationship for a moment? In a world full of choices and commitments, friendships can be a tug a war, or just a flip of a coin. Love sometimes brings out the best and worst in all of us. Dudley finds out the hard way that no matter how much of your heart you put in it, someone is always on the opposite end, trying to ruin your moment. Love or lust, people will do anything to be happy or just get what they want out of love. Some of the best things in life are lost moments; once love is gone, you may never get a second chance, you can only look in the rear view as love pasts you by.

Chapters

1. Communication

2. Can I borrow a dollar?

3. Training day

4. Rain Check

5. Bad Weather

6. Enough is enough

7. Actions speak louder than words

8. Trust me

9. Guilty

10. Prayer changes things

11. One hand washes the other

12. Return to sender

13. Last night of freedom

14. Endless Love

Chapter 1 – Communication

It's Friday night in Baltimore City, and there's an Over 21 and Fly partly going on off of North Eutaw Place. Of course, ladies get in free, so the fellas know the ladies are going to pack the place. Dudley Keys has been planning this night out with his boys for about two weeks now. His girlfriend Porsche Randals also has been planning for this event and neither has communicated with the other about going. Porsche's already pissed off because Dudley will be starting a new job a few hours south in Virginia. Though he's planning to come home on the weekends, for the past two weeks, conversations between the two have often been bitter or whispering silent. Dudley has been walking around the house complaining of not getting enough affection from Porsche, and she has been making it worst by walking around the house naked at times, just to tease him. Porsche often sleeps on the couch after watching re-run episodes of Atlanta House wives, which really pisses Dudley off.

The other day Dudley made it home before Porsche, and decided to start the week off right, He cooked her favorite meal, rented a few movies and threw a load of clothes in the washing machine, so that when she arrived from work, she could relax. Of course things don't always go as plan, Porsche called Dudley, and said she would be making a stop after work to pick up a few things; Dudley tried to hint to her to hurry home. Instead, Porsche, hangs out for nearly two hours with some girlfriends after work, for happy hour. With all the music playing, she never noticed the nine missed calls she had received from Dudley. By the time she did notice, she was getting into her car three hours later headed home. She didn't think anything was wrong, but decided to call anyway. The tone Dudley used to answer the phone wasn't very pleasant. "Where the hell are you at?" Stop cursing at me Dudley, said Porsche. I went to happy hour with Phontay and Riley. Time just went by so fast. "You been drinking?" said Dudley. "A little", said Porsche. "Why isn't that when I ask you to drink with me, I'm considered an alcoholic, but it's cool to drink with your friends?" Before Porsche could start a sentence, Dudley slammed the phone down. Mad as hell, Porsche calls back; but, the line is busy. Dudley had taken the phone off the hook. Porsche just wanted to get home, she was tired and tipsy.

She made sure the numbers were hidden in her purse before Dudley found them. Some of the guys at the club were all over her and her girlfriends. Porsche loves attention.

As Porsche pulls up to the apartment, she notices every damn light on in the place, and you could hear the music from the parking lot. Being funny, Dudley put the chain on the door. So she repeatedly rang the door bell. After about six rings, Dudley slides the chain off and opens the door. Not wanting to add more fuel to the fire, Porsche, zipped past Dudley, threw her purse on the couch and went into the bedroom. Mumbling under his breath, "I bet you are tired", Dudley continued in the kitchen packing up all the food he had just cooked. Porsche walks into the living room with a blanket and pillow, and positioned herself on the couch. Dudley slams the dishwasher door, left all the lights on, and went into the bedroom. Before he decided to go to sleep, he locks the bedroom door, as if he was teaching Porsche a lesson. This is not the first time something like this has taken place, but it's usually followed by one of the two, giving in or before the night is over, their sexing each other like two wild pit bulls in a cage. Not this night, both refused to give in to the other. Porsche texted every guy she met that night, as she laid on the couch alone. Only one guy responded back and they texted each other for hours.

The alarm clock goes off at 6:00am, like clock work every morning and without it, both Dudley and Porsche would be late everyday. Dudley turned down the alarm last night, so only he could hear it. As he opened the bedroom door quietly, Porsche, still feeling last night, was snoring as if it was the weekend. Dudley, jumps into the shower, and followed his everyday routine trying to make sure Porsche doesn't wake. He didn't know she had a company meeting that she had to attend at 8:00am; but, even if he did know, he felt this was a lesson learned for her. Its 7:25am, Dudley decided to skip breakfast, and made his way out the door, while Porsche still slept in her same position on the sofa. As he walked to his car notice a business card at the front door of Porsche's car. It read "Snake" a male exotic dancer and on the back of the card, it' read, "Please call me anytime". As innocent as it looked and seem, Dudley placed the business card on her windshield, but only after he had wrote, love Dudley on it.

"Ring, Ring", Porsche jumps from her sleep, scared by the loud telephone ring. "Hello". "Girl why are you still at home, the meeting is starting in five minutes, and I've called your cell phone about thirty times". "Oh shit", "girl what time is it", "it's 7:56", "damn it!" "Dudley wake up, wake up Dudley", she hollered, "Girl let me call you back".

Porsche runs to the bedroom to wake up Dudley and the room was empty, Dudley was gone, "That no good nigga", as she raced to the closet, trying to piece anything that looked like an outfit together. "I can't believe that fool wouldn't wake me up, as important as this meeting is to me". Standing in the bathroom naked, with one leg on the toilet, leg spread, washing between her legs, dialing Dudley with the other hand. Of course he didn't answer, and she didn't have time to leave a detailed message. You would have thought she was superwoman, as fast as she put on her clothes, she still wouldn't make the meeting. Half way to her job, she notice blue lights behind her, she was being pulled over by a cop for speeding.

Once Porsche got to work, her boss immediately signaled her to his office, everyone had a look of shame on their faces. Shutting the office door behind her, her boss Mr. Eric Stanton, explained to her that mandatory meetings are for everyone, and if you can't make it, you must call. Before she could explain, He slid a pink note to her, "What's this?" "I'm suspending you for 3 days, unpaid for your actions". But, Sir I over slept; I promise this will not happen again. Mr. Stanton wasn't trying to hear no excuses. Her eyes full of tears and anger; she signed the paper and walked out. Everyone pretended they were working as she walked towards her area. Her girlfriend Phontay asked was everything okay, but, a pissed off Porsche, didn't even hear her, and walked to the exit door. You could see people whispering, "Did she just get fired?" Once on the elevator, Porsche called Dudley's job. The secretary answered and said Dudley was in a meeting but would be going to lunch soon. As Porsche said "thank you" politely, Phontay called in, "Girl what's going on?" "Dudley didn't wake me this morning, He got dress and left for work and didn't wake me". Girl that is so fucked up, did they fire you? No they didn't. "We had a fight last night, it's my entire fault, I should have come straight home after work, and I feel really bad". "Why"? "Well Dudley had fixed dinner; the room smelled like roses, and I'm out drinking with you bitches". "But on the other hand I'm pissed, because I just got suspended from work for not attending the group meeting and it's all that nigga's fault". "I'm headed to his job to confront him". "Girl now you know you shouldn't do that, that's that man's job you fucking with". "Hell he fucked with mine". Then I'm going to make his punk ass give me some gas for driving for 2 hours to confront his ass. Porsche I really think you should calm down, it's not worth it, at least you still have your job, plus you need a vacation. Vacation my ass; I'm tired of his shit. "Okay be careful, you know that nigga is going to flip on you". If you need me call me. The whole time Porsche was driving she didn't realize the business card on her windshield. As she stopped to get gas, she took it from the wipers and read what Dudley had put on the back of it. "Keeping doing dumb shit, I'm going to sleep with him", as she mumbled under her breath in a low tone.

As Porsche pulls up to Dudley's job, she notice him standing in front of the building with some chic, who was smoking a cigarette, and he was waving his arms as if he was explaining something to her. She could see the female nodding her head as if she understood. At first she thought about just sitting there for a moment, but her patients was wearing thin. Porsche brought attention to herself by blowing the horn once. Dudley looked up, and motioned to the female, that he would be back in a minute. At first he thought about getting in the car, but quickly changed his mind and walked towards the driver, side window. "Why can't you get your ass in" said Porsche as she, rolled her window up. "Why are you coming to my job with an attitude?" Porsche didn't say a word. Dudley slowly walked over to the chic he was talking to and said something; she walked off in a bit of a rage. He got into the car, without causing a scene. Porsche pulled off just as he was closing the door, and immediately, she went off. "Why in the fuck did you leave without waking me up, now my ass is suspended from work for missing my group meeting?" "You being suspended from work, what in the hell does that have to do with me?" Dudley sat quietly; he didn't apologize or even look Porsche in the eye. "Are you finished?" "It's not my fault you didn't put your job before partying, so don't come with that it's my fault shit". "Lately all you seem to ever think about is your job and your friends, why are you in a relationship, if you're not relationship material?" Porsche just stared out the driver's window, speechless. "Just what I thought", said Dudley. "Maybe I need to give you some space". "I've decided to take the job in Virginia, so I'll be coming home on the weekends". "So you made a decision like that without consulting me first"? If I don't look out for my future who will? "I fixed you dinner last night to discuss the pros and cons of taking the job, and I had to give them an answer this morning, you was unavailable last night, so I made a decision independently, since lately you've been undependable", said Dudley. Infact you didn't discuss with me that you were going to be home late, I mean you could have atleast dropped me a phone call. "Look after work I'm going to the gym, so I'll be home later"." I think we need some time apart". Dudley don't talk that shit to me about time apart, your ass ain't going no fucking way. Porsche you better start respecting me and stop talking that bullshit to me. Oh by the way, did you get the stripper dude's business card, you dropped it getting out of your car last night. Dudley exited the car. Porsche rolled down her window, can you give me some gas for bringing my ass all the way out here. Hell no, nobody told you to come to my job, he said. Porsche just sat for a moment; then made a phone call, "Are you busy, can I come over and talk to you?"

Chapter 2- Can I borrow a dollar

Since all of Porsche's friends were at work, she decided to go to her old neighborhood where she grew up, on the south side of Baltimore. She just needed to talk with someone, plus she needed some money. This was not the perfect choice, but her ex-boyfriend, who she would conversate with every blue moon, seem to be the only person available. Plus he was a street nigga, didn't work, but had a little money coming in from hustling the block. He always had a thing for Porsche, but after years of verbal and physical abuse, she had enough; but, always found herself back in his circle. It was not like he had shit or had shit to offer, he was just something to do, down time you can say.

As she drove through the neighborhood, she spotted a few childhood associates she grew up with. Several of them where on drugs, some selling drugs and some never seem to find their way out of the hood. Pulling up near her ex's place, she noticed a female sitting out on the porch and then Block came out, handed her something and she left. *Oh Block was his street name, that's what everybody called him, the kind of nigga that would do anything for a dollar, no big threat, but he would get over on you if he could.* "Girl getcha ass out the car", nigga I'm coming don't start that shit, damn. Walking quickly towards the door, trying not to be seen by anyone. Block was standing in the door, drinking a beer. As soon as she walked passed him, he smacked her on the ass. "Nigga will you stop it?" "So who was that bitch, some crack head gone wild", said Porsche. "That was my money why, anyway what's up with you, you trying to get back with a nigga?" Block asked. "Nothing and I know you wish I was, I just got suspended from work, and I need a few dollars to put in my pocket". "You and that nigga broke up yet?" said Block. "No", Porsche said. "So why you didn't get it from his simple country ass?" "What that nigga got that I don't have, you know I still want you". "Yes I know, you text it to me every other day". "So what's up then", "you know we will always be cool, but we had our time together, you put me through hell Block". "I've changed", "you haven't changed, and you still got that foul mouth and have a very disrespectful attitude nigga". "All I need is $200.00" said Porsche. "I can pay you back next week". "You can pay me back right now", said Block. "You know I love sexing you". Porsche just rolled her eyes. "Why everything got to be about sex with you, why can't you just look out for me sometimes?" "Girl when I was looking out for you, you were sneaking behind my back fucking with that country boy you with". "Oh shit here we go again, why you can't just let it go nigga". Block grabbed Porsche by the hand, pulled her close and started kissing on her neck. She didn't show that much of a resistance her nipples were getting hard through her shirt. "Have sex with me, and you don't have to worry about paying me back". At this point she knows if she doesn't he would soon act up, especially when he has been drinking all day. "I promise you one thing, we are not about to make this a habit, and do not try and blackmail me either". Block just stood there smiling, grabbing his crotch. She slowly walks towards the bedroom, as Block finishes the last beer sitting on the kitchen table; you go smoke this blunt with me when we're done? "Now that's what a nigga like to see", as Porsche ignored him walking away. He already had his clothes halfway off as he entered the room. "First give me the money, before you even see this pretty pussy". "Damn you don't trust me", "hell no I don't, this is only business". "How much extra for head", "nigga I'm not putting my mouth on your stanking ass dick". Porsche gets the money, secure it in her purse, and gets naked. Block watched every piece of clothing removed from her body, as if he was in a candy store. To arouse him alittle, she smacked her ass a few times before getting on the bed. Lying on her back, Block slowly started kissing on her; she felt a lot of guilt. Block was busy enjoying giving her oral sex, he was handling her so rough, but overcoming the smell of his alcohol was the worst. "Will you hurry up and cum", "stop fucking rushing me". Do you have a condom, for what, because I said so, or we can stop, "okay let's stop and give me back my money?" She knew she needed it. Come on nigga, let's just hurry up. Porsche lay on the bed covering her breast with one hand. Looking up at the ceiling when he was on top of her, made her feel cheap, he was fucking her with no care, smelling like liquor, as he started to masturbate, he bruised her left breast squeezing so hard leaving finger prints. It was just sex, is what she kept telling herself, she pushes him off her as he went to the bathroom to quickly wash up. While in the bathroom, the phone rung, Block was still naked lying on the bed, he didn't pick it up, but a female left a message. "Block I had to rush out this morning to get to work and left my panties in the shower, will you put them in the hamper for me". Porsche heard the message, so you fucked someone last night or this morning and just fucked me. Bitch you know I fuck other broads don't act like this is breaking news to you. You're the one who needed the money, I hope like hell you don't give me shit. Bitch please, you called me. Okay I got your bitch, I'm out, peace. Porsche put on her clothes to leave, tell that nigga of yours don't eat you for a few days, unless he wants my cum in his mouth. Fuck you Block. "You just did" he said. Porsche slams the front door as she exited. Walking towards her car, she saw this truck with 30 day tags ride by, hit the brakes, but kept going. She started to get nervous because people in the neighbor knew her. She cranks up the car and speeds off quickly. Her cell phone had 13 missed calls from Dudley. She didn't even stop for the red light daydreaming on the mistake she just made. Dudley had left a few messages, but she was too scared to even check them, plus she was racing home before he got there, to take a shower. Porsche wasn't even paying attention to the stop light she just ran; luckily no one was coming through the intersection.

Pulling up to the house she notice Dudley wasn't home yet, so see quickly made her way to the bathroom to take a shower. While taking off her clothes, her girlfriend Phontay called. "Porsche, where have your ass been?" "Hold on, let me put you on the speaker" said Porsche. I'm trying to get undress. "Dudley has been looking for you, and he sounded a little pissed off to" said Phontay. "Girl, I needed some money, so I went over to Blocks". "Block!", "I thought you wasn't fucking with him", "I'm not, but you know he wanted some pussy", so I fucked him right quick and got paid. Now I'm getting in the shower before Dudley get home. You better hope, Dudley doesn't find out, and he won't, men don't have that gift to cheat like us hoes do, "laughing". Bye girl. (Click) Porsche jumps in the shower. Dudley slowly walks out of the lining closet; he had a look of hurt and anger on his face. He heard the whole conversation. He purposely parked his car in the garage and hide once Porsche came in the house, he's intention was to scare her. He searches for her purse, finds the money and hides it in one of his suit jackets. The shower water stops running, Porsche was in the shower singing, he shuts a hallway door to indicate he had just arrived home, "Porsche?" "I'm in the bathroom". Walking in the bathroom, he could barely see Porsche's face, the steam was thick as fog, she was butt naked wet, and it took all he had to hold back. "I'm going to run to the store to pick up some food, what you want?" "Whatever you get is fine", Porsche said. Damn can I get a hello with a kiss, a slap, a kick, maybe a punch. "Yea I want to slap your ass alright" he said. He quickly grabbed his keys. As Dudley left the house, he held back from knocking out her car windows. She made sure he was out of the garage before she made a move. Porsche grabs her purse and stuffs it in a lock safe she keeps on her side of the closet. She lays face down on the bed feeling miserable about what she had just done.

Dudley calls his brother, and told him what just happened. "Bro, all I can tell you to do is confront her about it; but, expect the worst. "Never be a fool for gold." He said. Whatever you do, do not put your hands on her, you have to know when to suck it up and walk away. At this point Dudley had lost his appetite; he hung up from his brother and just sat in the parking lot of WAM Burger Joint for a few minutes. He did manage to pick up some food, and make it back to the house.

Walking in the house, he could hear Porsche hanging the phone up. Dudley puts the food on the table; Porsche walks in the kitchen wearing nothing but bra and panties. Normally when Porsche has done something wrong, she became very talkative and sexual. Dudley remained calm, though inside he was boiling hot. As she started fixing the food, Dudley walks to the bedroom, picked up the phone and pressed redial. One, one, one, appeared, she had erased whoever she had dialed, and the caller i.d. was blank. So many red flags were there, but time after time, he was willing to forget all that had happened. Not this time, this time was different, he had proof from the horses mouth. Walking back into the kitchen, Porsche was stuffing herself with food, "what's going on with you, you're acting strange" She said. "Nothing much, just looking forward to starting my new job", said Dudley. "When are you going to start?" said Porsche. "Not sure", said Dudley. "I'm guessing in about two weeks". "So tell me how is this going to work or are you going to drive from Virginia to Maryland everyday back and forth?" "We discuss this already I'm going to stay in Virginia during the week, and come home on the weekends; do you have a better suggestion?" "Would you like to relocate to Virginia?", "I can't I have my job here, and I can't go anywhere else making the salary that I'm making". I knew you would say that anyway, I just ask to see what lie you would tell. "How do you know that if you don't try anyway, you need to learn to step outside of the box". *(The telephone starts to ring)* Porsche answers it, "Hello", "Dudley it's for you". "Hello", "thanks, I sure can, and I look forward to it". *(Click)* "What was that all about?", "that was my new manager, and I'm starting my training Monday, from 9 to 5 in Washington", "Monday, my family reunion starts Monday remember". "So I guess you're not going to Colorado with me this weekend?" "I can't now, but I can fly there Thursday night, training is only three days". "Ok, I guess I will change your flight then". "Before I leave you need to pay the phone bill, I am tomorrow, and I'm going shopping in the morning for a dress for the dinner in Colorado". "Why are you buying a new dress, with all the clothes you already have", "because I want something new". "I hope you're not going to charge it on the credit cards", "No I got cash", "how", said Dudley. "You don't get paid this week, and you just borrow a hundred from me two days ago". "Dudley please do not start with me". Porsche gets up and walks out the kitchen, to the bedroom. Dudley started getting flashbacks of the phone conversation, and the money he hide from her purse. As he entered the bedroom, Porsche was curled up under the covers, reading a book, you know I think starting to live them characters you be reading about, who's the author of that book you reading? A.Dakala, you should try reading some of his novels, please I will pass that's girly shit. Dudley lies beside her, not with the intentions of having sex with her, but just to see how she was going to react. Why in the hell do you have on perfume? I can't get in my bed smelling good, or is that your punch line to start an argument? He started kissing on her, as she started to gentlely push him back, "not tonight Dee, I'm tired", "tired of what, it's not like you worked today". "I just got a lot on my mind". "I'm sure you do", Dudley said as he rolled over and closed his eyes. Inside Dudley was pissed, wanting to say something so bad, but he kept his mouth close. Porsche laid there with the book still in her hand, I think she may have read the entire book twice making sure that Dudley wasn't trying to get in her panties tonight. Lord knows her pussy could not take two beatings in one day.

The next morning Dudley got up early, over in the night, he had time to think about how things were going with him and Porsche.

Chapter 3- Training Day

Training day comes, Dudley has packed all his bags, Porsche was suppose to go to work today since she was off her suspension and was coming back home before Dudley leaves to see him off. After waiting for about an hour, she never shows up. Dudley calls Porsche at work, but no one has seen her this morning, and she's not answering her cell phone. So he writes a note, and takes his bags to the car. Lately Porsche's actions hasn't surprised Dudley at all, he has gotten use to it.

Porsche was in a board meeting at work and couldn't leave, but she did manage to call Dudley at home with the only 3 minutes she had to go to the bathroom. No answer, Dudley had already gotten on 95 heading towards D.C. As she walked back to the meeting, she asked one of her assistance to call Dudley's cell phone and let him know she was in a meeting and couldn't leave, but will call him this evening. Dudley never got the message from his music blasting in his vehicle.

Once at the training facility, a group of twelve individuals were introduced, all new hirers. All expected to get to know each other over the next 3 days. As the managers proceeded talking about the company's goals and agenda, Dudley noticed there were only two blacks in the program. Himself and a young beautiful black female that seems to have a serious look on her face. They went around the room and introduce themselves. The last person to introduce herself was the young black female. "Hi, I'm Troyia Patterson, originally from Baltimore, but

I live in Washington D.C, I have no kids, single and currently pursuing my master's in Business". Dudley tried his best not to stare, as she took her seat, her eyes, glanced at Dudley, and showed a slight smile. After the meeting, everyone headed to lunch, and then would have the rest of the evening to themselves until training starts tomorrow. At lunch, Troyia was sitting at a outside table alone, talking on her cell phone, Dudley walks over and ask could he have a seat. "Sure", she responded. "Girl, I will call you later tonight, and hung up the phone". "How are you", Dudley said. "I'm good, how are you"? "I'm good". "So you're from Baltimore, what part of the city", "Southside, Brooklyn area". "Okay, cool and you". "Well I'm from the Eastside, but I live on the Southwest side near Catonsville". "Okay my moms live in that area, so you visit Baltimore often", "not as often as family would like". Said Dudley. "So are you married, Dudley", "no I'm not married", "I have a friend, she's from the Brooklyn area as well". "Oh really, a friend, what's her name, Porsche Randals". "Do they call her Shay", "yes, you know her?", "I use to, we grew up together, she use to hang with my brother's wife"."We all use to be tight, but life grows up" said Troyia. "You still talk with your brother's wife", "yes, we best friends, her and Shay I meant Porsche use to be best friends". "So, when is the wedding, what wedding?" "I don't see us getting married". "I don't see us together another month, in fact we may have broken up when I left for this training". Porsche never could seem to keep a man any longer than a year. "She still thinks her shit doesn't stinks", Dudley couldn't help but laugh. "Yes she still conceited", "how long have you been with her", "we been together off and on for about two years". "All I can say is be careful have you and Block had it out yet?" "No we haven't", "well don't be a fool; she's still sleeping with him". "How do you figure that", "I'm not telling you this because I hate your girlfriend, but she will sleep with anybody's man who shows her ass little attention, money or if she thinks he got money"! "Infact, she only got with you, because she either thought you had money or you getting money". "Her and block was made for each other, He use to beat the shit out of her, he had 2 or 3 kids while he was with her". "She scared of his low life ass". "Let me stop fronting on you Dudley, I know all about you and Porsche's relationship, my best friend told me you had got the job here and that we would be in training together". "I promised myself, I wouldn't get to close to you, and let you know that I knew you or her". "I've heard only good things about you; you work hard, love hard, and put up with a lot of shit from her". "I think you're a good looking guy, and a woman like me who's looking for a good man would die to have a man like you". "But, don't be a fool for gold". "Damn, you are the second person that has told me that in two days". "I'm go be straight up with you, and I'm not saying this for you to run back and tell her I said this", "I would never do that, said Dudley. "The other day, she was over Block's house, he gave her some money and fucked her". Dudley didn't look surprised at all, remembering the conversation from the closet. "You better watch her, Block fuck with a lot of tramps from the hood; she grew up lying, and will always lie". "I'm not the type that will go try and sleep with you, because I hate her, but, some black women have a good man, but rather settle for trash". "Troyia, I respect all what you're saying, a lot of it I know already, "but we stay together, and I'm using this job to get me to the next level, and she's not included in that plan". "I know about her going over to Blocks, I was home and she didn't know it, and I over heard her conversation". "Do you know her girlfriends Phontay and Riley"? "Yes I know them, Riley doesn't really fuck with Porsche cause she knows Porsche has sleep with Phontay's ex-boyfriend, but she has never told her, that's why you don't see her around a lot". "You're right, so why is Phontay and Porsche so close". "From what I was told, they both had a lesbian experience together, and one is scared the other will tell". "You know I've heard stories about that, but at this point it doesn't matter, I got to do me". "Well don't let her bring you a STD", "well we don't even have sex, it's been months since I've even touched her". "Anyway enough about my personal life, what is there to do around here"? Troyia responded. "I'm sure there's a lot, but remember we have training in the morning, so you better get your rest". "I think I'm going to grab a few movies at the red box, and call it an evening" said Dudley. 'If you don't find anything to do and would like to come watch a movie, I would love the company" Dudley said smoothly. "What time are you talking", "whenever you finish checking in with your girlfriend" said Troyia. She gets up and walks away smiling, "what room are you in, 2305"said Troyia.

Dudley calls home, Porsche picks up on the first ring, "what you doing" he said. "I just got in the door, I was running to the phone", "sorry I missed you before you left, I had a board meeting". "How was the training" said Porsche, "it was cool, long", "any other blacks in the group", "yes a black female" said Dudley. "Oh, so are you going to get to come home each day", "No they want us to stay in D.C. then I will be home Friday evening, and start my job in Virginia that Monday". "What room are you in"? Said Porsche, "I'm in 2301", "what hotel", "The Hyatt" responded Dudley. "Don't be having any bitches in your room", "Girl please.

"Porsche why are you cheating on me"? "What are you talking about, I'm not cheating on you", "and you would testify that in church?" "Yes", "Girl you going to hell for sure". "Listen I know about you going over to Blocks, and I know about the money he gave you". "I overheard your conversation, and I've been told by your haters". "So you're going to believe them over your girl"? "Yes, I believe you over yourself, because I heard it from your mouth as well". Porsche sat on the phone silently. "I would be silent to, I've giving you nothing but the best I could, and I still have to deal with the lies, and other guys". "Enough is enough, you're going to miss me when I'm gone, I promise you, you will". Porsche hangs up the phone!

Chapter 4- Rain Check

Troyia had picked up a few movies, she really didn't think twice of Dudley coming over to watch some movies, but thought it would be good if he did, though she was a little bored. As she was walking back to the hotel, along the boardwalk was a few guys sitting on a bench talking, she could hear them whispering compliments about her body, and just smiled as they spoke. One of the gentlemen was very aggressive with his approach, "what's your name love", "excuse me?" "What's your name", "no what's your name", "I'm Carlos", he said. "Hi Carlos, I'm Troyia". "I'm in bit of a rush, nice meeting you", "we haven't met yet", "if it was meant we will again" she said. Walking away, Troyia knew he wasn't her type, maybe a few years ago, but that wanna to be a thug act wasn't her vision in search of her knight in shining armor.

Walking towards her door, she notice a note on her door, it was a brief not from Dudley. "Troyia, not sure what time you were available, but if you want to watch movies early, I will be down at the pool". Troyia quickly made her way inside and changed into some comfortable boy shorts and grabbed a towel. As she approached the pool, she notices those same thug guys lending over a fence talking with some females lying in the pool chairs. She laughed to herself as Dudley spotted her, and motion for her to come on in the pool. Looking at Dudley without his shirt on, she was highly impressed, and as she got closer, she didn't look too bad to him either. I'm not sure if his eye balls or his smile was the biggest. Troyia had every man at the pool scoping her out, as she removed her towel, and sat on the side of the pool. Her breast looked so firmed in your bathing suit. The guy she met earlier walked behind her and offered his phone number. Dudley had just come up from under the water. Politely Troyia said "sorry, I'm on a date with him", pointing at Dudley, "sorry dude, I didn't know"," it's cool, who can resist a beautiful woman like her, I'm not mad at you" Dudley said smiling. Dudley and Troyia, died laughing. Greeting each other with a hug first, Dudley embraced her so tight as if he wanted her breast against his chest. "So did you check in with your girl first", "why you have to go there, I don't check in", "if you were my man you would". "Oh really, Dudley smiled". "Is that an option?" Troyia just ignored the comment and changed the subject. "So are you coming in the water?", "well I don't won't to get my hair wet, plus I'm tired". "So why did you come down", "well I got your note, and I wanted to see you". "Thank you for coming'. Troyia got down in the water, within 15 minutes in, it started to rain. "Oh shit, my hair", quickly she jumped back onto the concrete. 'Let's take it in and watch some movies, I'm not trying to get sick out here". Dudley, slowly put his towel around her shoulders as they walked towards the hotel. Standing behind her watching her hips move, he could only smile. "I can dry off in the room; I want to take a shower anyway", "me to" Dudley said. "What time do you want me to come over?", "why can't you just come now", "I have to take a shower", "shower in my room, we grown, I won't bite, plus we just watching movies". Well I wouldn't won't you to get all aroused seeing me naked", "Dudley please don't arouse yourself with the thought of me looking at your naked ass". "Plus I've already felt your eyes on me since you seen me". Dudley was speechless. "See you in a few minutes boy", she said. Dudley went to his room to grab some clothes and forward his calls to his cell phone.

As he walked back into the room, he could hear Troyia's cell phone vibrating, bouncing off an empty glass near the lamp. Whoever it was really trying to get in touch with her, curious Dudley picked up her phone, and it said Jason. The water in the bathroom stopped running, "Dudley are you in there?", "yes, waiting on you", "you can come in; I told you I won't bite". A nervous Dudley walked into the bathroom. It was steamy; Dudley stared as he watched Troyia behind the stain glass shower glass, turning the water back on, starting to wash her body. Her breast was the perfect size, from the side, he could see the frame of her ass, firm, thick, and she had no stomach at all. He didn't know whether he should take off his clothes or wait. "So are you getting in?", "I was waiting on you". "Boy get your ass in here and wash those nuts". Slowly, Troyia pulled back the shower curtain, not ashamed of her body; she continued to wash in front of Dudley. As she bent over to wash her ankles, her breast just hung at a perfect level, nipples hard as the water dripped like the seconds of a clock. "Oh, by the way, somebody name Jason was blowing up your cell phone". Troyia just laughed, "Don't worry, that just my little brother, he's in college". "So Dudley, do you mind washing my back for me?" Dudley washed Troyia's back, scared to go near her ass, but she insisted he washed lower. "Now turn around and let me wash your back", she said. To make Dudley even more nervous, she grabbed his penis, and began washing it, he got aroused quick. "Boy let me stop you getting hard too quick; I don't won't you to think you getting some ass". Dudley looked stuck as she exited the shower. "So we can watch a few movies before you get sleepy." "I bet you'll fall asleep before me", "you got a bet". As the water stop running, steam made it hard see through the bathroom mirror into the bedroom. Troyia was busy returning the phone call from Jason. Dudley could only hear Troyia cursing at the top of her lungs, repeating, "Nigga I told you its over, stop calling me!" Then the phone slammed! Dudley continued to dry off, 15 minutes later he walks out of the bathroom. Troyia had the lights off, there were two candles lit, the radio was playing very low and she was sipping on a wine cooler. "Damn you must have been dirty as hell', she said laughing. "I've been waiting on you for almost thirty five minutes". "I had to make sure I was fresh". "So did you call your brother back?" "No it wasn't my brother; it was my ex-boyfriend Jason who called". "Oh, so you still have feeling for him", "no, he won't leave me alone; I'm done with the drug dealing type guys". "I called him back when you got in the shower". "Thank you for being so honest with me, I over heard you cursing him out". "Your ass was ease dropping on me", "yes I was a little" Dudley said. Troyia threw a pillow at Dudley as she set up in the bed smiling. "I do have a brother name Jason in college though, so I want to clear that up now". Troyia had this devilish look in her eyes as if she wanted to jump in Dudley's arms. Quickly Troyia mood changes a little as Dudley picks up his cell phone, "No that tramp didn't call", Troyia said smartly. Dudley pulls back the covers and before he could get in bed good, Porsche calls. "Damn, I knew it would be too good to be true". "Hello", Dudley said in a low tone, Porsche was screaming on the other end about Dudley not calling her. After about five minutes, Troyia got from under the covers and put back on her panties. Porsche was still fussing, Dudley's eyes was focus on Troyia, because she was waiting in bed butt booty naked, until Porsche called. Dudley rushed Porsche off the phone, talking in codes. Porsche said she was not trying to get off the phone, and if Dudley hangs up she would be driving to D.C. Dudley hangs up the phone anyway. Porsche calls back about a dozen times. Troyia reaches over and put his phone on silent. Troyia, turns her back to Dudley, "why you so far away from me", "cause I'm sleepy". "So now you don't won't to watch a movie, because you mad?" "You sure you'll be able to watch a movie without any interruptions?" Motionless Dudley gave a quick moan, slowly sitting up right in bed. Troyia turns over halfway to watch the T.V., then reaches over and turns off the radio. "You can get under the covers if you're cold", Dudley pulls back the covers. "So you were naked waiting for me", "no I wasn't naked for you, that's how I sleep", (clinching the covers up against her breast) "Baby, be yourself around me, sleep in what you sleep in, we not having sex anyway." Dudley slumps down under the covers.

After a few hours of laughing and watching movies, Troyia said she was sleepy. Dudley turns off the Television, as the two lay there in silence. You could hear the echoes of someone banging the headboard against the walls from the next room. Troyia pushed her body towards Dudley. He pulls her hips closer to him, slowly kissing her neck. With one hand, she slides down her panties, kicking them to the bottom of the bed. Dudley sits upright, as Troyia turns and start to kiss Dudley's chest, while helping him take off his boxers. Her breast felt warm against his body, as he stroked his hand through her braided hair, his penis was waiting like a batter in the batter's box. Dudley placed a finger under her chin, pushing her head up, kissing her on the forehead. Troyia falls back slowly, pulling Dudley towards her, as her legs were wide open. Without any direction, Dudley slowly proceeded to enter, but Troyia, stopped him, "No let's just enjoy foreplay, I'm not ready for sex yet". "Where's your condom anyway?" Dudley went limp a little, but couldn't resist kissing Troyia's nipples. She soaked up every moment of it. Moaning every time his tongue licked her nipple. Her vagina was soaking wet, as they both just enjoyed being against each other without intercourse. Dudley placed his head on her chest, just listening to heartbeat. She took your nails and massaged the back of Dudley's neck. They both just laid there in silence. Someone started banging on doors down the hallway, it was so loud, infact it soften the mood a little but laying there in each others arms, was just what Troyia needed. The loud banging put both of them to sleep. Dudley had a hard time closing his eyes, thinking that it was Porsche knocking on doors, a few minutes later dismissing the thoughts, slowly falling asleep.

Chapter 5 "Bad Weather"

Troyia's alarm clock sounds at seven o'clock loudly. A few moments later the telephone rung, there was a message stating that the training session for today has been cancelled due to the bad weather. With the training cancelled, this means a free day to mingle. It didn't take much to get Troyia in the mood, as she slowly pulls Dudley to the bed. Her moans where like walking in a darkroom crying for help. She was like a dog in heat, not having sex in months really began to show. Dudley was taking every stroke in strive, as he pin her hands over her head, sucking on her breast continuously. Troyia's orgasm came so quickly, it was so warm, as she grabbed Dudley's neck to embrace him, but he wasn't finished. Slowly with so much intense, he enters her vagina, Troyia clutches the pillows, pushing her open thighs, closer to Dudley. Sex started to become a workout, Troyia arches her back with every stroke. There were moments of silence, then an outburst of relief. "Damn, I came again, boy what are you trying to do to me", as she wiped the sweat from Dudley's forehead. Dudley rests his head on her breast, slightingly kissing around her nipples. "Dudley you are addictive", as he lay there wore out and tired. In a calm rugged voice, "what would you like to do today?" Dudley said. "I wish we could just lay here", Troyia said. I tell you what let's ride to Baltimore and walking in the Harbor.

Dudley makes his way back to his room, there were a note taped to the door from Porsche. Dudley looks around to make sure she wasn't about to knocked the hell out of him. Entering the room, he notices a familiar smell of perfume that he has only smelt on Porsche. As he set down on the bed to read the letter, Troyia knocks on the door. "Is everything okay, yes I got a note on my door from Porsche. "Oh really", she says she will be in the parking lot waiting to see what bitch I'm with. "Whatever, that tramp don't won't none of me". Dudley I need to know what you are going to do, stay with her or be with me. Honestly Troyia, I want to be with you, Porsche and I have been over with for months now, I'm tired of the fighting, the lies, plus she cheated the whole time we been together. Well you need to break the news to her today when we get to B-more, or I will.

The rain was coming down so hard. So let's drop my car or your car off at my place in D.C. then drive to Maryland, Dudley agreed. Troyia had already packed her things; she sat on the edge of the bed angry, as Dudley packed his things. No one was saying a word, "Calm down Troyia, let's not spoil our trip together", Troyia didn't say a word, then Dudley's cell phone rung. He tried to ignore it; Troyia didn't hesitate to answer it. "Hello, Hello", an unsure voice responded back, "may I speak to Dudley"? Who's calling, his girlfriend, "wrong, you mean ex-girlfriend", Troyia said. I'm his new girlfriend. Porsche was in the middle of saying

something, when Troyia hand Dudley the phone.
"Yes Porsche", who in the hell is that bitch
answering the cell phone I bought you? Porsche
listen, I'm coming to get my clothes, you been lying
and cheating on me for months. I guess you thought
I wouldn't find out about the money from your ex,
you sexing him, and there's plenty more BS. I've
found someone who wants a real relationship.
"What you mean you found someone, I wish you
would show up her to get anything, I will have your
ass locked up". Damn you Dudley and that whore
you with, if she shows up at my house I'm go beat
her down. Porsche hangs up.

Once Troyia's car was dropped off, she seemed
to be in a better mood. Dudley walks around and
opens the door for her; she just smiled, leaning over
to push his door open. There was no mention of
Porsche the whole trip to Baltimore. Troyia's cell
phone rung, but she wanted Dudley to answer it, but

by the time he did, they had hung up. Someone left a message I guess, my code is 1971, and you can check it. Dudley didn't waste any time to do so. It was some guy name Drew, saying his boy wanted to meet you this weekend, call him. Dudley hands Troyia the phone. She didn't explain, she started dialing Drews' number. "May I speak with Drew?" "Hey Drew, yes I got your message, listen thanks but no thanks for the hook up, but I'm happy with the guy in my life now". Drew was on the other end getting a little loud, Dudley grabs the phone, homeboy I would appreciate if you would stop calling my girl. Drew hangs up. Troyia leans over and rested her head on Dudley's arm. He reaches out to hold her hand as they entered into Maryland.

Chapter 6 "Enough is enough"

Pulling up to his house, Dudley notice the parking lot was full of cars. Troyia started taking off her earrings and putting her hair in a ponytail. Dudley told her to stay in the car, she really didn't want to, but she did pouting. Before Dudley could open the door, Porsche's ex-boyfriend opens it. He was there with his brother and Porsche had one of her girlfriends there. As he approached Porsche, he mumbled, "I see your ass didn't waste any time", Dudley walks into the bedroom, Porsche followers him, pushing him in the back. He grabbed what he could and exited to his car. Everybody in the house came outside; Troyia was still sitting in the car, and just hoping someone would say something to her. As soon as Porsche spotted her in the front seat, all hell broke loose. "I can't believe you had the nerves to bring a bitch to my house". Troyia jumps out the car eagerly with fire in her eyes, "Who are you calling a bitch Porsche?" Damn and the witch even know my name. Then Porsche's eyes got so big, she couldn't believe it was Troyia. Yes it's me, so who's the bitch now. Troyia walks up to Porsche, "You're a dirty as broad", first you pretend like you in love with Dudley, sexing your ex for money and I guess you thought my cousin wasn't going to find out about you sleeping with her man. Porsche was speechless; I mean she didn't say one word to Troyia. The girlfriend that was there was Troyia's cousin. "Porsche tell me this is not true", Phontay said. Porsche walks away; Phontay gets in her car and drives off. Dudley just sat in the car and let Troyia say what needed to be said. Block the ex never came out the house. Porsche walks over to the drivers window crying, telling Dudley how sorry she was and please don't leave her. Dudley starts the car, never letting down his window, Troyia gets in, and he drives off, glancing back in his mirror, watching Porsche falling to her knees crying. Dudley turns up the radio; every other song was a sad love song. Troyia knew that he was hurting inside, and allowed him to vent. "Are you going to be okay", she asked. I'm okay I'm just disappointed in myself for allowing this to go on so long.

Finally back in D.C, the rain had stop just a little. Baby do you want to just leave your things in the car until tomorrow morning, and we'll come get them when we wake up. Okay.

Inside Troyia's place was very upscale, nice leather furnisher, very clean, and smelt like fresh cinnamon. Dudley, smiled as he looked at some of her baby pictures. "Girl, you had some big ears growing up", "whatever", she said laughing. So do you have a big family, "yes?" You will get to meet some of them tomorrow, we going to go over to my moms. Make yourself at home, what do you want to eat, I'm not hungry at the moment, can we watch a movie and chill? Yes we may, so what are you going to do about living arrangements, not sure, I will start looking tomorrow. Why can't you move in with me? Dudley, tried to changed the subject, so what do you have to drink, Dudley don't change the subject, I would love to have you here with me, if you want, I don't won't to rush you. Let's talk about it tomorrow Troyia. So what movies do you have?

Troyia had prepared a nice dinner, as Dudley flipped through the channels, sipping on some wine. Someone was ringing the doorbell, Troyia openings it, it was her sister Tina, and not realizing Dudley was there. "Girl I heard what went down", oh excuse me I didn't know you had company, Dudley this is my nosey as Sister Tina, Tina this is my Dudley. Hi Dudley, can I call you Dee, sure you can, and the two extended hands out to shake. So what's for dinner, girl you know I make myself at home when I came through. So Dee, do you really like my sister, Yes I do, you not going to hurt her, because we got crazy uncles. Dudley just laughed no cause I would hate to hospitalize one of them uncles. Oh you got jokes, I like you already, girl he a keeper. Thank you sis, but I've already made that decision, I'm just tried of his ex. Troyia, I thought we wasn't going to talk about this right now, you right, I'm sorry. Well, I won't to talk about it, Tina said, is she a problem, because we eliminate problems around here. Calm down Tina, Dudley said, things are okay, so who is this bitch Troyia. I'm not going to say, I promise my man I wouldn't talk about it, but holler at me tomorrow and I will tell you. Troyia could sense she was making Dudley a little frustrated, so she changed the subject. Tina's husband called to check on her, and within thirty minutes, Troyia's whole family was there to greet and meet Dudley. You would have thought it was thanksgiving, but Dudley was comfortable, as the men talked sports and the women talked Dudley. Troyia, wasn't trying to give out too much of her business, but did share they had a lot in common. The guys had been drinking for hours at this point. The door bell rung! Tina answers the door, Troyia ex-boyfriend Jason walks in without asking. Hey everybody, baby I just got a call from the Dallas Cowboys, I report to training camp next week, now I can put you in that big house you always wanted. Dudley stood up; you could hear Tina saying, "Oh shit", one of the Uncles grabbed Dudley motioning him to sit down. How you go come over here unannounced, there are no more us Jason, I've told you this, Troyia said angrily. Baby, calm down, let's go in the room and talk. "Hold up partner", Dudley jumped up and said. "It's over between you and her", "who are you"? "I'm her new man", "so you got seconds to leave". Everybody, stopped whatever they was doing, the room got silent. Jason and Dudley were staring at each other, it seemed like minutes. Dudley politely walked to the door and opens it; you have 10 seconds to leave. As Jason was walking out, he started mumbling, she's going call me as soon as your ass isn't around, and she loves money and materialistic things. It's you or a pro ball player, and partner you will lose her in the end. Dudley slams the door behind him. Troyia grabs Dudley and pulls him in the bedroom, everyone talked among themselves.

Troyia was crying, why are you crying, cause I don't won't you mad at me, why would I be mad at you Troyia, it's not your fault he came over. I love you with all my heart Dudley, and finally I'm happy. Jason is crazy, baby I'm crazy to; I'm not worried about that fool. Stop crying, Dudley wipes the tears from Troyia's face, kissing her lips. Tina knocks on the bedroom door, "are ya'll okay". Yes we okay Troyia, said. As they walked out of the room, one of the uncles put his hands on Dudley's shoulder and whispered, "Anytime you want to break that niggas ribs, let me know", you can always count on us, just treat my niece right and make her happy. Troyia got on her cell phone and called the police about taking out a restraining order out on Jason.

Chapter 7 "Actions speak louder than words"

Last night was a long night; Troyia's family didn't leave until about two in the morning. Dudley was still sleep, as he rolled over to hug Troyia she wasn't there. He could hear someone moving throughout the house. Baby, as he called out twice, "yes" she answered back, but sounded like she was in a closet. What are you doing up? Dudley gets up; Troyia was standing in the hallway, with nothing but thongs on hanging up all of Dudley's clothes. "Good morning Baby, I hung up your clothes and everything in the bathroom on the left is yours". Wow, you're looking sexy and you been busy, yes I really couldn't sleep, and you got drunk with my brothers and uncles. Did I really, yes I had to walk you to bed. I wanted to sex you last night, but you just laid there. Dudley just smiled. But I did get me some oral sex though, "what", yes I sucked your penis while you were sleep, it was good to. Dudley puts his arms around Troyia, and kissed her neck. "Boy, go brush your teeth, your breath smells like old beer", as she just laughed. "Do you want breakfast?", "yes but let me fix breakfast for you", Dudley said. First I want to get in the shower.

Dudley's standing in the bathroom running his water to shower, Troyia's peeping through the bathroom door, watching Dudley undress. Slowly she took off her thongs, pushing the door open. Dudley had already gotten in the shower. She pulls back the shower curtains and got in. As she stood behind Dudley kissing his back, he reached back to squeeze her ass, she reached around to caress his penis. Dudley turns to face her. The water showered both of them like a waterfall, her breast were soapy, nipples pressed against Dudley's chest. He pulls her closer, palming both ass cheeks as if he were lifting her up. Troyia leans back on the wall, lifting up one of her legs, she whispered in his ear, no intercourse just foreplay. Dudley, drops to his knees, kissing between her thighs, a few minutes turn into an hour, the water got cold. "We got to stop", Troyia said. She pulls Dudley back up; both were still kissing and touching. The water got too cold, as they exit the shower, Troyia mention; she wanted to have a serious talk after or during breakfast. Dudley's eyes shared at Troyia as she dried off, the look he had on his face was that of a hungry child wanting more candy. "Why are you looking at me like that?" "I just love what I see", he said. "Would you like for me to finish drying you off", "No, because you will try and get some, and I'm hungry for some food". "I want you to fix me breakfast naked so I can watch you", she said.

Dudley started fixing breakfast; Troyia was reading the newspaper and flipping through the T.V. channels. Dudley really tried to avoid talking about anything personal, during breakfast time. He had one eye on preparing breakfast, and the other on watching Troyia. She was about to make her move, first she turns off the television, staring off into space for a few seconds, and the words rolled off her tongue. Dudley gasped for air, "Baby, how serious are you about me?" Troyia said. What you mean, I love you, why you asked. Last night, I couldn't sleep, I had time to think about my life and what I wanted in life, and you know, I want to settle down, have a family, be a wife, have a husband, you know. Dudley got a little nervous, I understand, but ….. What's the rush? There is no rush, but we're getting older, I don't won't to wait until I'm thirty five to be just getting engaged to get married. "So let me ask you, how long do you think it takes for a couple to know If their ready to settle down with each other?" Dudley paused; let me think about that one, tell you tomorrow, no I want an answer now! Well I think a couple would know within the first year, I agree, so tell me, when did you realize Porsche wasn't the one for you? Honestly after a couple of months, I started to see things I know that would be a challenge. What things? Let's eat and talk before our food get cold. Troyia, couldn't wait to hear this. "Okay, it's like this; we never could get on the same page after the first date". After a month together, she needed money to go see her brother in jail, so I rented her a vehicle to travel in. The trip was only 200 miles, enterprise didn't have unlimited miles for that weekend it was only 500 free miles. Anyway, when she got back and I returned the car, I had to pay more because she went over the 500 miles. As the car rental employee was cleaning the vehicle, he ran inside and asks me did I want the camera and brochures I left in the console. The brochure said Sea Winds Resort in Myrtle Beach, South Carolina. "So I asked her how did you go over 500 miles on a 400 mile round trip?" She started to make up things, and all I heard were excuses. I found out that her and her girlfriends went to Myrtle Beach for spring break bike week, on my expense. I could never trust her again. "So you stayed with her because of what, sex?" "Yes and No", I stayed because I thought I could change her, the sex was okay, we would have a good week, then a bad month. I kept giving her chances, but in the back of my mind, I knew she would mess up again. So everytime we would had intercourse I would make sure I wore a condom. Sometimes you got to know when enough is enough. "I feel you Dudley, I've put up with a lot with my ex-boyfriend to, he would go hangout at the strip clubs, then come home and want to have sex with me, so I just decided to stop having sex with him" Troyia said. "Even when we had sex I was a little reluctant, cause I really didn't know you, I just let my heart take over". "Troyia I've never had a STD and I don't want one either, but if you want to start having protective sex I understand". "I really think that would be a good idea, don't you think so?" "By the way, are you on any birth control pills?", "No I'm not, and judging how we have sex I better get on some or you going to be a daddy sooner than you want to be". "Do you want any kids Troyia, well I do, but I would like to get my career started first". Dudley, what are we going to do about us working at the same job? Honestly, I haven't thought that far ahead, this job means a lot to the both of us, do you think we can manage working together and being together. It would be hard seeing some broad all up in your face if she's trying to talk to my man, but I wouldn't get upset at work. I say we try it for the first few months and see how it goes. That sounds good then if we needed to make a change, we will sit down and talk about it. "Okay, baby I'm going to lay down", "lay down", "yes", "I didn't sleep last night", "what, you did with all that loud snoring". "That's because you had things on your mind, and you was drunk", laughed Troyia. Troyia walks in the bedroom and shut the door, Dudley was left to wash the dishes, "can you at least help me wash the dishes?" he said. "Just leave them until later, come get in the bed with me", Troyia hollered loudly.

Walking into the bedroom, Dudley's cell phone started to ring, it was Porsche. "Dudley I really need to talk to you in private, can you meet me today?" "Porsche, I really don't have much to say to you, why you want to talk now?" "Look I know I made alot of mistakes just let me explain to you, please". "No I don't think that would be a good idea, I will call you back later, I will have to see". "Okay, okay" she said. Dudley walks into the bedroom, "who were you talking to?", that was Porsche calling. "What did bitch want?" "She asked if we could talk to me today", "about what", "I'm not sure". "But I do need to get the rest of my things from the house". "So you're going to get them today", "I would like to". Troyia turned over and put the covers over her head. Dudley reaches over to hug Troyia, but she didn't want to be bothered.

Chapter 8 "Trust me"

Dudley got up from sleeping nearly three hours. Troyia was also still lying down. As he was looking through his closet, Troyia wakes up, so you're going to get all fly just to go get your things? No, I'm not getting fly, but I need to put on some clothes. "Why didn't you ask me to ride with you?", "because I know she wants to talk, you don't have anything to worry about", "I'm not worried, that bitch better be worried about me". Troyia picks up her cell phone and calls her girlfriend. "Girl, what are you doing today?" "Nothing at all", "me either, well come by I'm here, I'm about to pick out some clothes now", "okay bye". Dudley was just staring at Troyia, what was that all about, nothing, your going to Maryland so I'm going to go shopping. "What time are you coming back?", Troyia said. "I will be back around 5 o'clock or before", "why so long Dudley?" Its 1 o'clock now, you know what, I will give until 6 o'clock, and if your black ass is not back it's on, and I better get a couple of phone calls from you. Troyia, please let's not make this a bad situation, trust me, you have nothing to worry about. Dudley starts to iron his clothes, Troyia goes in the bathroom and plugs up her curlers. So Troyia what are you putting on today? "Clothes", she said *smartly shutting the door forcefully*. Dudley shakes his head as he walks into the bathroom to get water for the iron, Troyia was sitting on the toilet. Dudley, I don't won't you to think I'm trying to be a bitch about this situation, but I know Porsche, and I know she got some shit up her sleeves to piss me off. "Troyia, you're not giving me any credit of being your man and knowing that she is up to no good". "I'm not about to jeopardize what we have I promise". Troyia, jumps in the shower, Dudley picks up his phone and calls Troyia's uncle.

Dudley was about to leave the house, Troyia was sitting in the living room, polishing her toe nails, Dudley reaches over to give her a kiss, she turns her cheek, save that kiss for tonight. It didn't surprise him of her reaction. Dudley walks out the door. Troyia was still upset that he was leaving without her. A tear formed on her cheek like a crystal diamond, then dropped to her shoulder like a water balloon exploding.

What Troyia didn't know, Dudley called her uncle Bernie to ride with him just incase something were to jump off at Porsche's. Plus Uncle Bernie wanted Dudley to take him to pick up his vehicle at the Jaguar dealership out in Catonsville. Troyia, called Dudley, "Dee, I was just calling to let you know I'm leaving with Misha", "okay so where are you headed?" "I'm going downtown, do I need to pick up anything for you", "no but baby I will be home before or by 6 o'clock". Okay I love you, love you to bye. Uncle Bernie gets in the car, what's up young buck, I'm good, and boy I'm glad you called me. So what's up with this ex-girlfriend of yours, man I don't know we been on the outs for months, and I just want to get the rest of my personal things, but I know she may have her people there. "Well I got my pistol because Uncle B. doesn't play, my niece will tell you about me". Dudley and Uncle B. really had a man to man talk, straight forward. Uncle B. explained to Dudley that Troyia has been trying to get away from Jason for years. After she got pregnant a year ago, Jason said he wasn't ready to be a daddy, so Troyia didn't want to do it alone and decided to have an abortion. Jason didn't even want to give her the money, but that's my favorite niece so I paid for it. I've never like that boy since. How can a grown man not want his child I never understood that. Now he trying to get into the NFL, and he thinks Troyia wants his money, my niece is smart, and she just wants to be happy. Money can't always make you happy, people has gotten away from real love. "So Dudley, what are your plans for my niece?" Uncle B. I truly love Troyia, want to settle down and start my own family, Troyia and I have so much in common. I know she got a lot of pain from the past, I mean even when I left the house, she was mad because I didn't ask her to ride with me. But I know she's been hurt and I'm not trying to hurt her anymore, I really love her. Dudley I'm 48 years old, I've been married for 22 years, relationships are complicated, but not impossible. You get out of it what you put in it. Four things to live by and I promise you and Troyia will be very successful. Communication, honesty, love and respect, Conquer those hurdlers and you can live happy. Oh, by the way, the sex has to be good to. But you have to make a woman feel that she's the most important woman in the world, give her attention even when she's not given it to you, the happier she is, and the more you will receive. Hell I'm 48, and I still get good sex from my baby. "Do you drink?", Uncle B. said, "Yes", "stop so I can get us some Liquor, if you wasn't with my niece I would take you to the titty bar, let you see booty", "Nah, I don't do strip clubs", "Got damn, my niece got you pussy whipped, that's alright". 'So what you drinking on", "whatever you drink I drink, you need some money?", I'm good, do you need a chaser or you drinking it straight, I can handle my liquor, I'll take it straight. Alright don't try and hang with Uncle B. and burst your heart, young buck.

Back on the highway, the two laughed and joked, the liquor was kicking in, but they were not drunk. Dudley pulls up to Porsche's, from the outside looks like no one was there, so he calls her cell phone, no answer. Since he still had the key, he decided to make himself in to get his things and leave. Uncle B. was right behind him, pistol in his pocket. As they entered the house Dudley called Porsche's name, no one answered. The house looked like there had been a house party last night. Dudley walks over the mess and turns on the bedroom light and screamed! Uncle B. runs to the room are you okay, yes, but look. There was blood everywhere, mainly in the bed and looked like someone got their ass beat, the walls had streaks of blood on them. "Look, we need to get out of here" Uncle B. said. What if someone is here hurt, and if they not, we could be the blame for whatever has happen. Dudley and Uncle B. didn't touch anything, as they were walking out; you could here a faded moan from a distance. "Wait, you hear that?" Uncle B. said, it's coming from the bathroom, but the door was locked. Dudley breaks down the door with his shoulder, Porsche was lying on the floor naked, covered in blood, she was not moving. Uncle B. call 911, said Dudley. Uncle B. ran outside to call dialed 911; Dudley continued trying to awaken Porsche. She just moaned in pain, there was a stab wound to right upper chest. You could hear the sirens from a distance getting closer. Dudley calls Porsche's friends, none of them answered there phones. The

Police and Paramedics arrived roughly at the same time. The police ordered Dudley to step back, there were six officers throwing questions at him at once, with guns drawn. He was trying to focus, looking around the room to find Uncle B., but the police had detained him outside. One officer walked Dudley outside for questioning; Uncle B. was handcuffed in the back of the police car. "Why do ya'll have him handcuffed, we are together", Dudley said. "Why do ya'll have a pistol with you, and we found open bottles of liquor in your car". "This is your car isn't it", one of the officers said angrily. "Yes, officer I swear we had nothing to do with whatever happens here, I use to live her, and I was coming over to get the rest of my things". 'Oh really, so when she wouldn't give them to you, ya'll raped and stabbed her". "Hell no, we ain't raped and stabbed no one"! The Officer wasn't trying to hear Dudley's explanation, he was handcuffed, place in a different police car. Both were taking to the downtown jail for more questioning. Meanwhile, the ambulance was rushing Porsche to shock trauma. She was going in and out of consciousness, but her injuries wasn't life threatening.

Troyia at this point is calling Dudley's cell phone, not knowing he is unable to pick up. With every call, she's getting madder and madder. As Troyia paced the floor at home accompanied by her friend Misha. Dudley and Uncle B. were being interrogated like murder suspects. Someone were ringing Troyia's doorbell. As she looked through the peep hole she realized it was her ex-boyfriend Jason looking as if he was high. "Troyia, I need your help", "What's wrong with you?" she asked. "Some dudes just jumped me and I need to call someone to pick me up". Troyia hesitated for a moment. "Okay come in, are you okay?", "yes" Jason said. "You got blood all over your clothes".

"They tried to stab me". "Look go into the bathroom, and clean yourself off, but hurry up cause I don't won't my man coming up in here and seeing you in here". Troyia, continued to call Dudley, his cell phone would just ring, then going straight to voice mail. Troyia left so many messages, that his voice mail was full. It was already six o'clock. "That nigga is an hour late; I'm go curse his ass out when he gets home". Misha, was just laughing, girl he might have just made a stop, what you need to do is get Jason out of here, that nigga crazy. Jason came out of the bathroom, "did you call someone" Troyia asked. "Yes my homeboy coming in a few". 'Okay you need to wait outside", "outside, why the hell I can't wait in here?" "Jason I let you in to clean yourself off and now you got to get the hell out!". Bitch you be tripping. I got your bitch stupid asshole. Troyia goes into the bedroom and grabbed a hammer. Jason walks out the door, slamming it behind him. She stands near the door to make sure he was leaving; you could hear his every step as it faded away. Then Troyia's phone rung, "Hello", "yes may I speak with Troyia Patterson", "this is her, how may I help you?" "Well this is Craig Pullman, I'm a local bondsman, and I got a call from your Uncle Bernie". "My uncle Bernie, about what?" "It seems that he and your boyfriend Dudley have gotten in a little trouble and being held downtown in the Baltimore jailhouse on attempted murder charges". Troyia dropped the phone. Misha picks up the phone, who is this and what's going on. She tells the bondsman they would be down there in about an hour. Misha tried calling everyone she could, no one could be reached. Within minutes everybody in the family started calling. Troyia was so upset, as she paced the floor, hands shaking nervously. "I know that broad had Dudley set up, but why was my Uncle Bernie there?" No one had any answers. They packed about four car loads of people and headed to Baltimore. The entire ride was in silence, Troyia stared out the window the whole trip up 95 north. Every so often she would wipe tears from her eyes. One of the cousins starting saying a pray out loud, then there were more tears falling.

Chapter 9 "Guilty"

Family and friends were still sitting in a waiting room at the jail, everybody wanted to know how Dudley and Uncle Bernie be charged with attempted murder and on whom. The bondsman was there, but he hadn't gotten any details about the incident yet. Aunt Cora, Uncle Bernie's wife was trying to console Troyia and keep herself together. Every thirty minutes, Troyia or Misha was asking the officer at the front desk, for an update. Dudley and Uncle Bernie had no idea that Troyia and the family was there, like protesters waiting to get answers.

Porsche had just come out of surgery, but was unconscious, she lost a lot of blood, right now her chances of making it is a fifty, fifty chance. Her family and friends has just gotten word of what happen. Porsche's brothers were mad as hell, ready to kill anyone that was connected to this; of course the first person that crossed their minds was Dudley. Once Porsche's family found out that Dudley was locked up, immediately her brothers were headed to the jail house, why everyone else left for the hospital. The strangest thing was no one has been able to get in contact with any of Porsche's friends at the moment. Porsche's aunt, more less big momma of the family, asked the doctors once they arrived did she have a cell phone on her when she arrived. But none of the doctors knew, one of the investigating officers came in to talk with the family. He wanted to know did she have any enemies, or a boyfriend. Porsche's family wasted no time in telling about the fight that she and Dudley had. The officer told the family that the neighbors said, *Porsche had a house party, and that it was more guys there than girls. As the crowd started to leave one guy was still there helping Porsche clean up. Now we just need to find out who the guy was. Do any of you have a number to any of her friends so we can start calling folks, the officer said. Oh, we have two guys in custody but I'm not sure are they connected, that's all I can tell you right now.* "Who are the guys?", Porsche's Aunt asks with tears in his eyes. "Sorry I can't say until the investigation is over with, I will be in touch with the family later today" he said. They tried to reach Porsche's brothers, making sure they weren't out doing something stupid.

Finally, the Patterson family was able to see Uncle B., only his wife was allowed behind the visitor's door. She was having a hard time keeping it together, Uncle B had this look of depression on his face, as soon as his wife sat down, and he started talking. "Baby we didn't have anything to do with this mess", "who is we Bernie?", "me and Dudley". "Dudley, Troyia boyfriend", "yes". Bernie explains the whole situation, which made a lot of sense to his wife. Well tell Dudley to hang in there we will get ya'll out of here. Bernie placed his hand on the glass, as his wife walked away. Once she got back in the waiting room, she explains everything to Troyia, now her anger turned into worrying. "Is Dudley okay", Bernie said he was holding up that they were interrogating him, trying to make him confess. How he going to confess to something he didn't even do, don't worry, we getting them out of here. The booking officer called Troyia and her aunt up front, the judge denied Dudley's bond, but Bernie's bond has been set at two hundred thousand. "What", why is it so high, well he's been charged for the loaded pistol he had and accessory to attempted murder. Dudley was denied because he was in the house when the police arrived, and if she dies, he could be charged murder. "Listen", the officer said, I'm not supposed to say this, but if they don't find any of his DNA linking him or have any witnesses that places him there, they will clear both parties. Troyia dropped her head, as the bondsman, placed his arms around her, you got to keep it together, and I'm willing to workout something to get your Uncle out, so let's talk.

Troyia's aunt refinanced their house to get Bernie out of jail, it's been a week now, Dudley is still in there, and Troyia has been unable to see him or talk with him. Troyia knows the new job is starting next week, and with all the news coverage,

Dudley will probably lose his job. Troyia has been trying to get the best lawyer possible, Dudley did have an opportunity to write a letter to Troyia, unfortunately she couldn't write him back. In the back of his mind, he feels he has lost her, and every minute behind bars gets harder and harder.

Troyia has spent of days just stuck in the house, reading the letter Dudley wrote. Her cousin that use to be good friends with Porsche calls her. "Hey Troyia" this Phontay, can I come over I need to speak with you. "Yes", Troyia said.

Phontay arrives at Troyia, hey cousin, hi, listen Troyia I want to get straight to do point, and whatever you need for me to do I will. Porsche had a house party at her place, even though I don't mess with her like that after she slept with my ex, I went anyway. There were a lot of guys there; one in particular that should out was your ex-boyfriend,

Jason. Are you sure, Jason, yes I'm sure, he walked up to me and said don't I know you; I said no I'm not from here. He said okay and walked away, but him and Porsche must have known each other, cause they greeted each with a hey boo, a hug then a kiss. The whole night they were arm and arm. All of a sudden, this girl walked in, saw Jason and went off on Jason, she and Porsche had so heated words. Porsche told everybody the party was over, so I was next to the last one to leave, expect Jason was there helping Porsche clean up. I asked her did she need anything before I go, she said no. When I got in my car, I notice all the lights in her house turned off, but her bedroom light came on. I know her and Jason was going to mess around that night. Girl and the strange then happen that night, Jason came over here talking about some guys had just tried to rob him, he was bloody, his face had cut marks on it, like he had been fighting. I let him go in the bathroom to clean up and he used the phone to call someone to pick him up. He got mad cause I wouldn't let his ass stay in here and wait, but I wasn't about to do that when I was expecting my man home soon. Phontay if I get in contact with the investigator, will you tell him what you know, I sure will. Troyia, called the officer, and he asked them to come down to the jail.

Downtown, the officer wrote down everything the girls told him, it was like pieces of a puzzle. Then the biggest break of all came, Porsche's next day neighbor found a cell phone lying in her front yard, and she said he recalled a gentleman that night searching outside like he had lost something, but when he notice her, he went back inside Porsche's house. The officers sent a patrol unit to the neighbors to pick up the cell phone. Troyia told the officer that if it's Jason, this is the cell phone number. Troyia and Phontay waited patiently until

89

the officers arrived with the evidence. Then one of the police officers called the cell from the police department phone, and it was Jason's phone. Now they had a warrant issued to question Jason. Troyia felt scared because she wasn't sure if he would come back over to her place, so she stayed with her cousin Misha for tonight.

The next morning, Troyia was awaken by her cell phone ringing, it was her Uncle B. telling her, the police had just arrested Jason down in Virginia at some motel. Also, Porsche had come through and was speaking with the police about what happen. Troyia jumped from her bed, are they letting Dudley out, I'm not sure yet, but they will be. Troyia calls the investigator. He explains that Dudley will be released in about two hours, and that Jason was being arrested for rape and attempted murder. She cried tears of joy; I'm on my way to pick up my man.

Dudley walked through the doors, news media, flashing lights, but all he asked for was his Troyia, they embraced, and a simple hugged seemed like minutes ticking.

A month passed, it was on every news channel and front page of every paper. Jason Gaddy was sentenced to twenty years in prison, Porsche made it out the hospital, but had to go through a lot of therapy, she eventually moved to Florida with some relatives, she and Dudley never talked again; in fact he changed his number so he couldn't be reached.

Chapter 10 "Prayer changes things"

Dudley lost the job he was in training for; Troyia still had her position, and was holding things down until he found something else. They decided to stay at Troyia place thought the job was in Virginia at least for another year, Troyia would just drive the forty five minutes one-way everyday until they were ready to buy a home in Virginia. Everyday seem like months for Dudley, every job interview resulted into background checks, though he was found not guilty, he had to get the charges expunged but didn't have the money to do so. Troyia seen the frustration in Dudley's action, I mean he didn't want to have sex, always in an ill mood. She knew he had a passion for cutting hair, so she took it upon herself to check on a few schools and what the pricing would be. Everyday she prayed for God to guide Dudley in a positive way, and help him work toward his goals and dreams. One morning Dudley got a phone call from a local barbering school about an available opening. Dudley was so excited; the problem was getting the money to start. He needed a thousand dollars. He wanted to tell Troyia face to face and decided to surprise her on her lunch break. For whatever reason Troyia wasn't at her desk, and didn't call Dudley once she got to work as usual.

Once he arrived at her workplace, he notices a guy who was in the training class with them. The guy told him Troyia called in and said she would be in late today. Dudley was a little pissed off, because she wasn't answering her phone, so he just sat at the back of the parking lot of her job, waiting for her to get to work. Within two hours, Troyia pulls up, she had a smile on her face, and she was fixing her lipstick and hair in the car. Dudley wanted so bad to get out the car and confront her but didn't know what he wanted to really say. Dudley felt maybe she was stepping out on him, because he wasn't working, and she was paying all the bills. It has been three months, since Dudley has worked. Troyia, gets out the car in a rush, and rushes to work. Dudley's heart was pounding, then his cell phone rung, "hey baby", it was Troyia. Hey, I've been calling you Troyia, I'm sorry baby, I came into work late today, I had to take care of some business, are you okay Dudley. Yes I'm good. Listen I'm just getting in to work, I have a lot to do, but I will talk to you when I get home, would you cook us a nice dinner tonight, I will be home around six o'clock, I love you, I got to go. Bye. (Troyia hangs up the phone).

Dudley drives to Troyia's Uncle Bernie's', but he wasn't home, so he just rode around for a hour, just thinking and thinking on how could he get the money to start school. He wanted to ask Troyia for the money, but felt less than a man asking his girl for the money, when she was paying all the bills. In his rear view mirror he notices a car behind him flashing their lights, and he didn't even know anyone in Virginia. As he approached the stop light, the car pulls up; it was an old childhood friend he grew up with in Baltimore. They pulled over and got out and talked. "Dudley Keys, what's up man", what's up Drew, man I haven't seen you since college. "I see you doing good driving that Range Rover", life is good still getting my hustle on. So what you doing for yourself, man, I just lost my job, trying to get on my feet. I can hook you up, and you can make some real money. Just take my number and call me tonight or tomorrow and let's sit down and talk, Okay, holler at you later. Dudley felt a little at ease, but still wasn't sure if he should take that chance, plus Troyia would be pissed.

Later on that night, Dudley had dinner fixed and ready. Him and Troyia love to play music around the house, Dudley was blasting the radio, so he didn't hear the telephone ring at first, but raced to catch the answering machine playing. It was her sister Tina, "Troyia, this sister Tina, did you meet with Black today, he was so excited about seeing you, let me know how things went." Dudley's heart downed, "I can't believe she would be cheating on me", is what Dudley was mumbling out loud. Just then Troyia walks into the house, hey Dudley, what you cooking. Dudley was silent, walking into the living room to turn off the music. Where were you at this morning? Damn, can I get a how was your day baby, I miss you baby, I told you this morning I had an appointment. So why did your sister call her about you meeting someone name black, just because I'm not working don't mean you have to go and cheat on me Troyia. Dudley I'm not cheating on you, "well who in the hell is Black?" Dudley please let's not talk about this right now, I just got off from work, and I'm tired. How you tired, you haven't even been at work a whole day, you didn't get to work until after twelve o'clock, I came to your job today, and you weren't there. I sat in the parking lot waiting on you for two hours. What do you want me to say; I told you I had an appointment. Well I came to tell you I'm going back into the streets to hustle, I want to go to barbering school and I need to come up with at least two thousand dollars. What you mean you decided, we didn't discuss this Dudley, I thought we were a team. In the mist of the argument, the door bell rung. "Damn we can't even have an argument without somebody knocking on the door", Dudley said. As she opens it, a guy walked in wearing a nice pin stripe suit, "how are you Mr. Warren", I'm good. Mr. Warren this is my boyfriend Dudley. Dudley this is Mr. Warren Black, who my sister mention on the answering machine, he's married to my Cousin Loretta. We call him Black. "What's up Dudley, you can call me Black as well, the reason I'm here is because I run the loaning department at one of the biggest banks in Virginia. Troyia met with me this morning, about a no interest loan, that I told her I could get approved for the both of you, if you still wanted the money to attend barbering school I can approve it right now for $8000.00 and ya'll would not have to start paying it back until you graduate school. Dudley looked at Troyia as if he was silently saying I'm sorry, Troyia's eyes got teary so she walked into the kitchen. "I tell you what, I will leave all the paperwork here with the both of you, just call me and let me know by Friday how much you need, and we can get the loan approve". Thank you Black, Troyia said, he then shook Dudley's hand and hugged Troyia. As Black left, Dudley just scratched his head, Troyia, listen I own you an apology. "Dudley you handle this situation all wrong, I was trying to surprise you, to lift up your spirits" and you just thought I was out cheating on you. I love you with all my heart, whether your broke or not, when I love I love hard, you mean the world to me. Baby I'm sorry, I just got so much on my shoulders, Dudley you don't think I don't know what you going through, I'm doing my best to hold it down for us, I don't complain about bills, I give you money every pay period, why would I cheat on you. Hell I'm waiting on you to propose, I would say yes and pay for the wedding. Troyia started crying, Dudley places his arm around her and just held her tight. Troyia thank you for all you have been doing, you're a good woman. So what do you want to do about the loan? *(Wiping her tears)* How much do you want Black to approve, well the whole barbering school is four thousand dollars, so how about we say, seven thousand, and once I graduate I will pay all of it back by myself. No I want to help; you are helping by being so supportive. Okay, but I'm willing to help when you need me.

Chapter 11 "One hand washes the other"

Dudley graduated barbering school, and already had a job in place. A lot of the clientele he built in barbering school followed him to his new location. The owner of the shop really liked Dudley, because he was always at work an hour before the shop open, and always the last one to leave. What made Dudley stand out over the other barbers was how he would market and promote himself. On his lunch break, Dudley would go downtown, and hand out business cards or flyers, advertising his skills. He even put up a big billboard downtown that was very visible to the eye of any out of towners visiting the city.

Troyia was so proud of Dudley, they had open there first bank account together. Troyia had a car payment every month, that she wished she could just get rid of, so Dudley would put up most of the money in their savings. Troyia's thirty second birthday was coming up real soon, and Dudley wanted to do something really nice for her. He started working at the barbershop every Saturday, and most Saturdays Troyia would sit in the shop with him like she was one of the barbers. She supported her man at everything he did, even taking it upon herself to be his personal assistance in times of promoting his business. His ultimate goal was to own his own barbershop. Troyia had a vision of being an interior designer but running her own boutique shop. He wanted to make sure her dreams came true as well. One of the shops regular customers, this female from the neighbor, would always bring her four boys in the shop asking for free hair cuts. She would always try to flirt with the guys, wearing short mini skirts with no panties on or low t-shirts with no bra on. Normally, the owner's son Clarence would cut her boys hair, but this Saturday, Dudley was the only barber on duty. The problem is, she pick the wrong barber to flirt with, especially with crazy about my man, Troyia being there. Troyia had went into the back room to get Dudley some fresh towels, when she returned, three of the boys were running around, and Dudley was cutting the oldest hair. Their mom was sitting in one of the empty barber chairs, leaning over towards Dudley. As soon as Troyia walked in, she corrected the whole scenery. She made the boys stop running around and their momma had to get out of the empty barber chair. Of course, that didn't sit to well with her, so when she asked Dudley who was she, Dudley proudly smiled and said, "That's my fiancée". You could damn near see the hard nipples through her shirt, go soft. I guess Troyia interrupted Ms. Thing's whole plan, it's not like Dudley would have even response to her anyway. When she left, Troyia looked at Dudley and rolled her eyes, Dudley smiled, hit her on the butt, then reached in his pocket and gave her all the money he had made for today to put in his money bag. Eight hours had passed, Troyia was getting tired and Dudley hadn't had a customer for the last thirty five minutes, so he decided to close shop early.

On their way home Troyia wanted to stop and look at the new Jaguar XF that just came out. Troyia went on in the car how she couldn't wait to pay off her vehicle, so they could purchase a new home. "Baby, how much do you owe on your car anyway", Dudley said. Not that much, how much, why? You scared to say, let's just say I got a bad deal on it, but I needed a car, so lord I'm not complaining. Okay I owe about nine thousand. Nine thousand, damn you have paid for that car about two times, laughing. Dudley don't be funny, I'm messing with you baby. As soon as we get caught up on some bills, we will pay your car off; in fact I will make this month's car note for you. Really, yes I will, so can I take that four hundred dollars and go shopping with it, Nope, you need to put three hundred of it in the savings account. Troyia's mouth was wide open. After leaving the Jaguar dealership, Dudley wanted to stop at the Honda dealership where Troyia got her car. "Sit right here baby, I'm going to make your car payment", Dudley said. But it's not due yet, I know we're just paying it ahead of schedule. Troyia sat in the car listen to her favorite song, "if I were a boy", by Beyonce. Inside Dudley spoke with the financial manager about the balance on Troyia car. He wanted to pay if off without her knowing about it. The finance manager said he could give Dudley a payoff of sixty five hundred if he paid it off today. Dudley pulls out his credit card and paid Troyia's car off. Everyone behind the counter smiled, that's a good gift for anyone. Now Troyia has no idea she has no more car payments. As he got back in the car, Troyia turns down the radio, so what's my balance now? Well they say you owe about eighty four something now. Damn, it's going to take me a year to pay off my car; I'm tired of car payments. Dudley just laughed. Once we get home can we stay in tonight, maybe order a movie, Troyia asked. Sure, what do you want to eat? Well I was going to fix us some shrimp that sounds good, do you want to invite your sister and aunts them over we can play cards tonight? That sounds good, hey we can do like a pot luck, everybody brings something. Okay I will call everybody once we think of a menu.

Troyia and Dudley love to entertain and host parties, but they always kept it family. A few guys at the shop wanted to go out to the club, but Dudley always said no, giving Troyia first suggesting at every weekend. Tina, Troyia's sister called and wanted to know did she want to go out with her tonight, she said no, I was about to call you cause we having a card party at the house, so come over, make sure brother in law comes to. Her sister went on by saying, he wouldn't be coming because he going out with the guys for the fourth weekend in a row. "Girl I'm so tired of his ass, all he do is go out with them, he spends no time with me", listen come over tonight we will talk. When Troyia hung up she told Dudley about Tina's situation, so they got into deep conversation about relationships. Troyia believed in that old fashion way of loving, the man is the head of the household, and the woman supported. Dudley agreed a little, but he loves everything to be equal, but agreeing the man should take the lead. He said, what Tina needs to do is put her foot down, tell him she's tired of him going out every weekend with the guys and not spending time with her. Obliviously he's not happy at home, because as men, we will stay home if there's something to stay home for. "But a man shouldn't have to have a reason to stay home with his woman when they are your woman", Troyia said deeply. "I totally agreed, because I just love being in the present of my woman", Dudley added. So is Tina scared to put her foot down, well I've heard that

Terrance has been abusive in the past, I'm not sure what's going on now, Tina only comes around when she feels like being bothered. So Troyia, let me ask you, do you think it's right for your sister or friends to call trying to get you out the house to party or whatever, when your happy in your relationship. No I don't think its right, because I know people will get jealous of your situation when their situation isn't as good. So why as humans do we go anyway, I guess because their family or friends and sometimes you just want to go to get out, but not with any intentions. It's like trying to please both sides of the fence, but personally I'd rather please my man, so I would stay home. Hell Tina tried to get me to go out tonight; I think she wanted to go see them male strippers. "Whatever", Dudley said, but if you wanted to go you can, I'll give you a few ones to put in them gay G-strings. Those guys are not gay, how would you know.

107

Troyia, leaned back in her seat and turned up the radio, Dudley just stared at her for a few seconds, then said, don't tell it on yourself, Ms. Innocents.

Let's stop at the store while we're out, so think of a menu while we are in here. Inside the store, Troyia ran into a guy she knew from College, she introduces him to Dudley, then he introduces them both to his wife. His wife was someone Troyia didn't too much care for coming up in college, but was very cordial with her. As they ended conversation and walked away, Dudley asked Troyia, what that was all about, what you mean, I sense you didn't care too much for her. "In college she thought she was the shit, sleeping with anyone's man, but I see she married the water boy of the football team". Not saying he not a good guy but damn she use to act like she couldn't be with a guy unless he was the most popular guy in the school. Calm down baby, Dudley said laughing.

Wine, beer, food, music and playing cards, that's all that was needed to jump off a good house party. Some were coupled up, some were single, but everyone seemed to be enjoying themselves, except Tina. She was continuously on her cell phone trying to reach Terrance. "Girl you going to let that man run you crazy, enjoy yourself", Troyia said. Dudley walks over and hand Tina a glass of Oak Leaf wine, it was him and Troyia's favorite. Thanks, brother in law. Troyia whispered in Dudley's ear to pull Tina to the side and talk to her about Terrance. Dudley politely motioned Tina to the hallway. Before Dudley could open his mouth, Tina started by saying, "why can't my husband be a good man like you"? Listen sis, I haven't always been the man I am now; a man is only as good as the woman he's with. I was in a very unhealthy relationship; it was filled with dishonesty, lies and no trust. Don't let your husband, deteriorate would God has created in you. Everybody look at Troyia and I and say, they have a good relationship, we do, because we communicate, we entertain each other; we share the good and the bad. As a man, when both of us having a bad day, I put my bad day aside to comfort her bad day. What I would advise you to do is, make him available to talk to you, tell him how you feel, and if you don't see changing results, you have to make your mind up is it worth staying in this. Tina's eyes never blinked, she soaked in everything Dudley said, you know your right, I'm going to enjoy myself and tomorrow I'm laying it all out on the table. Thank you Dudley I really needed to hear this, anything for my new family. "Tina, also, let tell you something in your ear", Dudley whispered something that made Tina smile from ear to ear. Troyia walked up, damn, what's so funny, girl you ain't trying to take my man are you? "I wish I had half the man you got" Tina said.

Thirty minutes remaining before midnight, and Troyia's thirty second birthday, she really didn't know this was a pre-birthday bash for her. All her family and friends were there. Troyia and Tina was on the card table, Dudley announced the winner of them game would get the one and only door prize, Troyia just laughed, what door prize, boy you drunk. Tina just looked at Dudley and smiled. It was the last hand, Troyia and Tina had just ran a Boston, Troyia slams her cards down in victory. "Alright, alright, let me have everyone's attention" Dudley said. "I want to continue partying tonight, but want to take this moment to say thank you to my new family and new friends". As everyone knows in exactly ten minutes, Troyia will be celebrating her thirty second birthday. So baby I have a few pre-gifts for you tonight." Troyia, was shocked. Dudley pulls out a dozen of roses and an over sized gift bag. Everyone was watching, no music playing, not a sound, Troyia slowly read the first card, and then she read the second card which had an envelope attached to it. Once she read what was inside the envelope, she started to cry, it was a pay off receipt for her car. "Baby you paid off my car", "yes". "Thank you, thank you, and thank you", she hollered. Wait there's more, Dudley went on by saying how Troyia has stood by him through his toughest ordeal, and he wanted her in his life for a lifetime, then he got on one knee, and said, "Happy Birthday, will you marry me?" Troyia damn near fainted, she said yes, then hugged and kissed Dudley, followed by bragging rights on the three carat ring he just placed on her finger. Tina looked at Dudley and smiled with a thumbs up. That's what Dudley whispered in Tina's ear earlier, she already knew about it.

Chapter 12 "Return to sender"

Troyia has been so busy planning her wedding, that's schedule to take place in less than two months, that most of the time her cell phone just goes straight to voice mail when Dudley calls. He knows she is excited about the wedding and Dudley on the other hand has been busy planning the grand opening of their first family business barbershop called "Just Cutt It". Since the wedding is coming up soon, Dudley plans to hold the grand opening a month after they return from their honeymoon. Thursday Dudley was scheduled to meet a few of his groomsmen to get fitted for their tuxedos; he was waiting on one other customer to arrive. The barbershop he currently works at is always packed on Thursdays with guys getting their hair cut before the weekend. So anytime a female would walk into the shop, she either knew one of the guys there or bringing a child with her for a cut. The guys were all talking sports when Dudley's ex-girlfriend,

Porsche walks in. Dudley stood there speechless for a moment, "hey Dudley, how are you"? I'm good, what you are doing here, I thought you were in Florida, I am. I heard you were cutting hair now so I just wanted to come see you and talk to you about our daughter. What you mean daughter, we don't have any kids, and Dudley I was pregnant when you left me for that tramp. Hold up, that tramp you talking about is about to become my wife. So I hear, so I wasn't wifey material? Listen I'm at my job, and I don't owe you any conversations, you made your choices, so deal with it. Everybody in the barbershop was quiet, even the kids there were tuned in. Dudley steps from behind the chair, and got up in Porsche's face; it's been a whole year and your not about to come up in here, talking about a child to me, you had me and couldn't keep me, move on. Everything that bitch is getting I deserve, so we can handle this maturely or through the courts, here's my number you need to call me, cause your child needs things. Hell I was with your stinking as for four years, you never talked about marrying me. Is that what this is all about, me marrying Troyia, I'm marrying real love, your love was fake and full of lies. Porsche throws her hand up in Dudley's face. As Porsche walks out the door, Dudley looked stressed, the owner of the shop walks over, "you can't turn a hoe into a house wife, you have a good woman in your life now, don't let what just walked out of here, mess up your happy home". Dudley left the shop early to go home.

Once he got there, Troyia was already home. When he walked in, she was sitting on the couch, as soon as he walked in, she hand him a letter. It was from the state of Florida requesting information on Dudley for child support. Dudley, I thought you and she were having protective sex; we were, so why is she claiming you got a daughter? Troyia I'm not sure, she even came by the shop today, and how she knows where I work I have no clue. Have you been talking to her, no baby I haven't and you know I haven't. Okay, okay, I'm not going to let this mess up my wedding day, we need to call whoever we need to call, and request a paternity test ASAP. In fact give me the letter I will make the arrangements. Did the tramp leave a number to contact her, I'm sure she did. Yes, give it to me! When Troyia called, Porsche's voice mail came on, Troyia made sure she left her number to call back. Within seconds she called back, as Troyia picked up a voice replied, "hey baby I knew you would call", "baby, bitch I got your baby, my husband isn't fathering shit you having". Whatever let me speak to Dudley, no you can't speak through me, and by the way I called and set up a paternity test for this Saturday at Sinai Hospital for 1pm, please be there, then hung up. Porsche called right back, I will be there bitch; you make sure your ass there. *(click)* Troyia there's nothing to worry about, I'm not the father, I promise you, and we always had protective sex. Dudley tried to change the subject, so I hear your dress is very beautiful, yes it is, I hope I get to wear it. Why you say that, because Dudley, I'm not sure if I could handle being married if her child is yours, as much as I hate that bitch, I would probably hurt her. Troyia you have stuck with me through so much, please trust me, she's just blueprinting a plan against me, because I'm marrying you. Well I'm not going to be able to sleep until this is over, this is the last chapter with her, and I still may whip her ass once it's over.

Troyia kept her word, she didn't sleep, and the bags under her eyes showed it at five o'clock in the morning. Dudley was still sleep, Troyia got up, turned on all the lights, doors started to slam, the television was loud. Dudley, slowly woken, one eye at a time, "Troyia, what time is it"? Time to get up, peeping over at the clock Baby it's five in the morning, what we getting up for, I want to talk before you go to work, get up. Dudley, sit up in the bed shaking his head, alright let me wash my face. By the way, I'm going to the shop with you today, so I can make sure we are at our appointment on time. Dudley walks in the kitchen, Troyia had coffee brewing and she doesn't even like coffee. She walked in the kitchen with a coffee mug, poured some in a cup, Troyia how many cups have you had, this is my six cup. Baby calm down, Dudley removed the cup from her hand, slowly kissing her neck, she had on only a wife beater, and her breasts were pressed against his chest. The palms of his hands embraced her hips like a NBA player gripping a basketball. She responded back by pushing her body closer to Dudley, now she could feel his penis through his boxers up against her vagina. He lifts up her t-shirt, caressing her breast, taking turns sucking on each nipple as she just lightly moan to every squeeze. With one hand, he slides down his boxers, until they drop to his ankles, then position himself to lift up one of Troyia legs, then the alarm sounded. "Okay time to stop" she said. What, yes we got things to do, you got to go to work. Baby, I'm horny, so am I but we got all day for that. Troyia walks out the kitchen into the bathroom and turns on the shower. Dudley leans back on the kitchen counter, looking down at his penis in disappointment, watching it slowly going limp.

Once they arrived at the shop, the owner told Dudley he had two messages by the phone. Porsche had already called there, Troyia was unaware of the messages, and Dudley decided not to even tell her, since things were already causing confusion. He just took the messages and threw them in the trash can.

Troyia brought a few novels to read as she relaxed by the television in the lounge area. Slowly each barber started coming in one by one, each greeting Troyia, each looking at Dudley smiling. One of the guys asked Dudley quietly, should I go back home and get my video camera, I feel like it's going to be a title bout in here today, then laughing. Dudley motioned with one finger over his lips for everyone to hush. Troyia walked in and said, "I wish she would come in here while I'm here today, I'm going to drag her up and down the parking lot". The shop erupted in laughter. "I'm going to get breakfast, write down what ya'll want", she said.

Troyia watched every hour go by, greeted every customer that came through the door. Dudley wasn't even that talkative today, of course with a girlfriend in the shop; the guys couldn't really talk about their normal topics, "Girls". It's just certain things women shouldn't and probably don't won't to hear. The shop got so crowded that you had now a lounge full of women, who either came with their men or bring their sons. So now the women had their own conversations going, but every now and then, Troyia would peek in the shop to make sure Porsche hasn't creeped in. Twelve o'clock came quickly; Dudley started packing up though he was planning on returning after his appointment, Troyia was on point, already with pocket book on her shoulder, walking towards the exit. She stood there patiently, as Dudley said goodbye and that he would be back shortly.

There were no signs of Porsche at first but then with four other females with her including a beautiful little girl in a stroller. They all were sitting in the waiting area, then the Nurse calls Porsche Randals and Dudley Keys. Troyia got up to and walked straight to the back with her man. Dudley went through the testing procedures as scheduled.

Troyia anxiety wanted to know how long the process would take to, the Nurse explained it would take three business days and they will call both parties in individual when the results are in. Troyia told the Nurse, that they could be reached on her cell phone and then they left. Porsche was still there, talking to the Doctor, she had the little girl on her shoulder. When Dudley and Troyia got in the car, she pointed out that the child doesn't even look like him. Dudley didn't say a word, he really wasn't worried. "I'm taking a half a day Tuesday when the results come in", she said. Dudley still didn't say a word. The whole ride back to the barbershop was silent, no music, no talking. Troyia still was pissed, driving roughly, on one occasion she ran a stop light without even realizing it. Dudley grabs his seat belt, oh you trying to be funny, she said. No but you driving crazy, slow your ass down Troyia! She hit the gas petal a little harder, going ten miles per hour over the speed limit of 65 on interstate 95 south. Out of no where the state troopers pulled up behind her, and threw on his blue lights. He motioned Troyia to pull over, so she did. Dudley just looked out the passenger window pissed off; the trooper wrote Troyia a one hundred dollar ticket for speeding. As she pulled off, she threw the ticket in the backseat. Please drop me off at the shop, or take me to get my car? "I'll take you to get your car, Troyia said. Once Dudley got his car, he called the shop to let them know he wouldn't be back in until Monday. For the next couple of hours, Dudley worked over at his new location, assisting the construction workers with a few minor things. Troyia went home, and position herself on the couch, reading her bible. She called Dudley three times, but he didn't answer. She knew he was mad and had a lot of stress going on, she wanted to apologize but was afraid, because she knew she was wrong.

The weekend went by so fast; I mean Dudley was on edge the whole weekend, Troyia, couldn't stop thinking about what if. It was Tuesday afternoon around two o'clock, Troyia's cell phone rung, it was the testing center; it was an automotive message saying your test results were in. Troyia's heart stopped for a second, she hung up hands shaking, and she slowly dialed Dudley's number. Dudley was cutting a clients hair when he got the call. "Baby the testing center called, the results are in, and do you want to meet me there"? Yes I will meet you there; I'm leaving soon as I finish this last cut. Troyia was in the mist of saying, I love you, but Dudley hung up so fast he didn't hear her.

Troyia walks into the waiting room and to her surprise; Porsche was already there with two other females, the child was even with her this time. Troyia tried her best to ignore Porsche and her friends, until she heard one of them say, "We about to get half of that check". Then Troyia stood up and said you wish you could, and then Dudley walked in the room. What's going on, I can hear ya'll all the way down the hallway. Porsche walked up to Dudley to explain, but he told her not to speak to him. Then a police officer came in the door. Everyone got quiet, but the officer wasn't there for them, he was also there to get test results for an inmate in the county jail. The nurse told the officer to come in, he wasn't there five minutes, then walked back out with a piece of paper in his hand. As he exited, the nurse called back Dudley and Porsche. Troyia again was the first one through the door. Doctor Agnes explained how the procedures work, and then told them the test results. "Porsche you know we tested both men", "Both", Troyia said. You didn't tell us there were two guys being tested, bitch I didn't have to tell you shit anyway. "Wait Doctor so somebody else was tested beside me", Dudley said. Yes you and a Mr. Jason Smith. Jason Smith! *(Jason was Troyia ex-boyfriend the guy locked up for raping Porsche a year ago.)* Dudley looked at Porsche and just shook his head. Troyia folded her arms and just mumbled, "once a hoe always a hoe". The Doctor proceeded with the results, Dudley you are 99.9% negative, Porsche, Jason was 99.9% positive. Porsche grabbed the test papers and stormed out the office. Troyia, hollered go visit your baby daddy in prison!

Chapter 13 "Last night of freedom"

This morning Troyia woke up vomiting, and it went on for a couple of hours. "Baby, wake up, baby wake up" she said in a low tone. Dudley jumped up; baby what's wrong, I'm not feeling good, I think I'm pregnant. Why do you say that, well I didn't won't to tell you until next month to make sure, but I missed my period last month. Do you want me to go get you a pregnancy test? "Yes". Dudley immediately got up and ran down to the 24 hour drug store on the corner. As he walked down the aisles looking for the pregnancy test, this guy walked by him, then came back and said "congratulations on getting married". "Do I know you", Dudley said. Well no you don't but we met briefly, I'm Troyia's ex-boyfriend and your ex-girlfriend's baby daddy. By the way, I didn't rape her, she was giving it to me when ya'll were together. "So what nigga, I got a good woman now", Dudley said and walked off. The guy stood there with his hands in his pocket. Once Dudley got back, he told Troyia what happen, she was shocked that he even got out of jail. She warned Dudley to be careful, that her ex was crazy as hell. Troyia took the test and went into the bathroom, after a few minutes you could hear her holler. Dudley ran to the door what's wrong, "Dudley we having a baby", Dudley jumped up, Troyia started crying, let me call my momma and sister. Dudley sat down besides her, rubbing her stomach, as she told her mom the good news. Everyone she called seem to be excited, things were falling into place.

Three days before the big wedding day, Troyia and Dudley were running around doing last minute preparations. Dudley was so relieved that Porsche wasn't pregnant by him and that Troyia was; now they could go on with their lives building their own families. Dudley was all set for his Grand Opening for their new barbershop after the wedding; Troyia had been promoted to Executive Director of Finance for the Department of Labor. Things were looking good for their future, now it was just a matter of getting this wedding done the way she wanted it. The only problem she was running into was finding a cheaper catering company. Everyone she called wanted forty five to fifty five dollars a plate pure person, and her guess list was well around two hundred guess. Tina was busy taking care of her bridal shower, which supposes to be about thirty females together on a dinner stripper cruise boat. Of course Troyia had no idea, and if she did, she probably wouldn't have approved of it. Dudley's best man had the bachelor party set for Friday, at one of Washington DC's most popular upscale stripper lounges. For two days Troyia ran down the rules of the bachelor party to Dudley. There are to be no touching, kissing of any sort on or from them hood rat strippers, Dudley just laughed, why you giving me rules, what about you? What about me, you know I don't do the stripper thing, and I hang with professional girls. Troyia who are you fooling; some of them girls are probably freaks. Stop Dudley no they are not why you say that, because you got a little freak in you, that's how we made a baby. Dudley reached over to touch Porsche's stomach; she playfully pushed his hand away, laughing.

It's Friday night, both Troyia and Dudley has been preparing for tonight, the wedding is tomorrow, Dudley is staying at his best man's house, while Troyia has a house full of females. They all were sipping on glasses of wine, even Troyia. Okay sis do not drink a lot tonight carrying a baby, I do not want to hear my brother in laws crazy ass go off and everyone made sure she didn't to. Why waiting on the limousine that Tina has picking them up, the girls exchanged stories about their favorite love movies. One of Troyia's co-workers, this white lady name Brandy talked about how her husband didn't want her to wear the jeans she had on. Tina asked her so how you convinced him. "Well I didn't, so I put them in my gift bag and changed in the garage". Everyone busted out laughing. Troyia had on some lovely House of De'reon jeans, a beautiful blue sweater and some two inch Gucci heels, that Dudley had to approve, just so she wouldn't hear his mouth she promised to wear them. Tina cell phone rings, okay the driver is here. Immediately all the girls pile up in the limo, the driver helped each one inside, when it was Troyia time; he gave her a dozen of roses, complimentary from the Limousine Company. The girls were loud and tipsy. Everyone was dancing in their seats to music blasting through the speakers. Cars would pull up trying to see through the dark tinted windows, on occasion, one of the females would stick her head up out of the sunroof. As the music went silent, the driver announced that they would be pulling up to the boat landing in two minutes. All wine glasses were turned up to empty.

As they got out the Limo, they were greeted by four guys wearing tight pants, no shirts and bow ties. Troyia looked at Tina, and all you could hear was, "Girls it's on now, damn look at his body". Walking inside the dinner area, you could see half naked men dancing naked on a make shift stages. Troyia tried to close her eyes trying not to peek at all the buff bodies and extra ordinary penises swinging around. They escorted the girls to their tables, Troyia pointed at a sign that said, "What goes on as a result of this boat ride, stays on this boat ride", her co-worker Brandy said "Amen".

Dudley and the boys gather up drinking before heading downtown, he knew that Troyia was haven't a good time, because she had not called. Dudley made sure he left his credit cards, and only took about two hundred in cash with him. In the back of his mind he knew Troyia would be pissed if she knew he was taking money to a strip club. All the guys piled up in about eight vehicles, all in single file line. The traffic downtown was terrible, and the ticket cops love putting boots on illegal parked vehicles. You could hear the music beating through the walls, as the guys walked down the sidewalk to the front entrance. Dudley almost got whip blash looking around at all the naked girls walking around. His best man had reserved the VIP section of the club; they were escorted by this five-five dark skin cutie that had an ass you could set a glass on. "So who's this special occassion for?" she asked. Dudley smiled from ear to ear, and then quickly raised his hand. She took him by the hand, his eyes were focus on the pink thongs she wore and walked him to the lounge couch he would be sitting in. Pushing Dudley down in his seat, she bent over to whisper "enjoy yourself in his ear", her breast slapping Dudley in the face. You could see him close his eyes as if he was in fantasy land. Soon after she left, ten more girls came in the lounge, followed by drinks and food. The party was about to start, Dudley's best man pulled out a money clip of twenty dollar bills. As the last female walked in the lounge, Dudley notices it was Porsche his ex-girlfriend. She tried her best not to even look at him. She immediately took off her top displaying all her breast as one of the guys in Dudley's group put a dollar in her g-string. She walked by Dudley, he reached out to get her attention but came up short, as another guy whispered in her ear and handed her some money. One of the girls closed the VIP lounge door, as Dudley was about to get his first private lap dance of tonight from his ex-girlfriend Porsche aka "Red Snapper".

The boat ride was about to come to an end, the girls were greeting the male strippers, some of the girls took pictures, Troyia said no, she only wanted to remember this night from memory. One of the male dancers really found Troyia attractive and offered to walk her to the car, after repeatedly saying she wasn't interested, he slipped his business card into her pocket. Once she got outside the door, she placed the card in the trash can without even looking at it. Inside the Limo, the girls talked about how the strippers were grinding on the women and soon the conversations switch to tomorrow being the big day. Troyia looked like she was tired; she said she didn't get much sleep last night. Her sister Tina and her best friend were staying over tonight with her. Tina hadn't heard from her husband all day and was a little worried, because they had another fall out this morning before she left. Before pulling back up to Troyia's place, she was telling the girls, she's thinking about filing for divorce because she just found out Terrance has a gambling problem. So this morning she froze their account so he couldn't take out anymore money and he swung at her, so she put him out. Troyia's co-worker explained that she went through the same thing a few years ago, that lead her ex-husband to doing hard drugs. The Limo then came to a stop near their cars, but Troyia first notice your brother in law, sitting on the hood of Tina's car. "Tina, Terrance is in the parking lot", oh shit she said. Don't worry girl we got your back, as they got out, Terrance walks up to the car, where's my wife. Troyia was shielding Tina, Terrance what's going on, your sister trying to stop me from getting my money. "Terrance I'm not giving you any money to go out and gamble with", Tina said walking backwards. He threw a beer can he had at her, but missed, but It got on Troyia, she quickly dropped her bag, and swing back, hitting Terrance in the lip. "Bitch" he said, and then pushed Troyia back into the Limo. The Limo driver reached under the seat and pulled out a pistol, while dialing 911. Troyia's best friend, picked up a brick and threw it, but missed. Terrance jumped in his car and left. Tina said she wanted Troyia to take out a warrant on him for pushing her, she said no, "I'm going to tell my man to beat that ass". After a few minutes and things calmed down, all the other girls left, but the police was still in route. Inside, Troyia had to be calmed down, she called Dudley, he answered but either could hear the other, where Dudley was at was so loud. "Baby I will call you back in a few minutes", he said. The 911 operator called back and said the police should be there in a minute, and then someone knocked on the door. "I think their here now at the door", Tina said. Without looking through the peek hole, she open the door, somebody rushed in with a ski mask on, Tina screamed as she was slapped with a metal object then fell to the floor. Troyia hollered, and then all you heard was three gunshots. *(POW, POW, POW)* Then the gunman ran out the door. Troyia was shot in the chest; Tina pushed her way over to her as if she was shielding her. Bleed was everywhere," call Dudley tell him Jason shot me" she mumbled. The cops heard the shots and was chasing Jason outside, they seen him running out of the building when they pulled up. One of the cops ran inside and called the ambulance. Tina was on the phone with Dudley, he immediately panic and was headed home.

Once the ambulance arrived they decided that the gunshots were life threatening, so they had a medical helicopter on the way. Troyia was still calling Dudley's name, Tina was being treated for lacerations to her forehead that required stitches. As the helicopter was landed in a field from the back, Troyia went into cardiac arrest; the paramedics were trying their best to bring her through. Dudley pulls up like a maniac and explains to the cops that she is his fiancée. "Who did this?" he hollered at the top of his lungs. Dudley wanted to hold Troyia's hand but all the medical personnel made it impossible for him to get to her. Instead he blew her a kiss. Before they could get Troyia to the helicopter, her heart stopped beating, then she stop breathing. Tina screamed, "Troyia", Dudley fell to the ground, a couple of the guys that was with him, dropped their heads. As Dudley got up and raced over to the stretcher, one of the cops was trying to hold him back. Seconds felt like minutes passing, as Dudley watched the paramedics like slow motion, pull a white sheet over fiancée's face. You could read the lips of one of the medical personnel, "She's Gone". She was pronounced dead at 2:47am, on the date of her wedding from three gunshots wound to the chest, one of the bullets pierced her heart. The race to at least save the baby was also unsuccessful. Dudley's face was frozen as he just stared without any emotions. No one made a sound, all you could hear was the sound of the sirens. The blood started to soak through the white crisp sheets that embroidered Troyia's lifeless body.

Chapter 14 "Endless Love"

It's been a week since Troyia's death, her ex-boyfriend Jason was locked up for her murder. In his confession, he wrote, he couldn't stand to see her marrying another guy and that he would have been heart broken for life. Dudley hasn't been the same since, he has spent most of his days, locked in the basement of his sister in laws house. He says it's hard for him to go back to the house, and will make plans to move everything out one day. Tina has been assisting him with the funeral arrangements for both Troyia and the baby, which Dudley named "Destiny". Tina had been saving the wedding gift that Troyia wanted to give Dudley on their honeymoon. It was a love poem she wrote to

Dudley and a two carat bracelet that read, "Troyia's king forever". *(Below is the poem she wrote)*

"Troyia's King forever"

I fell in love with your good side, your bad side,
your wrongs and your rights

Your smile, your laughs, brung my guards down
that night

Our first kisses lead us to drinking wine, then soon
making love

That night I dreamed of white doves, woke up in
your arms, tightly hugged

I prayed for true love God sent me a king to make it
better

So I gave you my heart in marriage, with a promise
to love you forever.

On the day of the funeral, Dudley spend the entire morning at the funeral home, sitting by Troyia's casket, talking to her about how their future would have been like. Every word was a struggle, as the tears flowed, followed by struggling smile. As he said I love you, he dropped his head in prayer, stood up placed a red rose in her casket and then kissed her lips. Walking away, each step was followed by a look back at Troyia as if she was watching him.

During the ceremony, family, friends and co-workers took turns exchanging stories of the girl a lot of people called the life of the party. Dudley spoke for about an hour himself, telling a standing church room of about two hundred people, what Troyia meant to him. His best friend stood beside him, practically holding him up from all the sadden emotions. She was dressed in her wedding grown, and looked as if she was sleeping peacefully. Dudley had huge pictures of her on each side of the casket, surrounded by dozens and dozens of roses and plants Once he stepped down, to close her casket, he reached in his pocket and pulled out the wedding ring, and gently placed it on her finger, every face in the church was drenched with tears, there wasn't a dry eye in sight, Even the Pastor had to be consoled. All of Dudley's groomsmen carried the casket out the church, Dudley and Troyia's mom just embraced each other all the way to the burial grounds. Sitting in the middle chair, surrounded by all of Troyia's family, Dudley reaches up and placed a picture that they took together and placed it on top of her casket. She was then lowered into the ground; you could see a sense of lost ness on Dudley's face. He then opens up a cage and released fifty white doves in the air. As the ceremony ended he shook hands and thanks those near him, as he walked alone back to the car, never turning to look back at the disappearing casket of the woman he fell in love with, Destiny La'Troyia Patterson.

- **Dudley keys**, would eventually over the next year seek treatment for emotional stress, he still to this day, owns and operates his own barbershop, which he renamed Destiny's Cutt, in memory of Troyia. He says he's not sure if he will ever date again, and has been practicing abstinence since Troyia's death. Recently he enrolled in a Bible College, studying to become a Minister

- **Tina,** Troyia's sister, finally divorced Terrance; he actually got locked up for five years, for assaulting Tina and Troyia that night. She almost finishes Cosmetology School, and will be working in the shop with Dudley once she graduated.

- **Porsche** still stripping at the club, she just had another baby, by regular customer of hers, twice her age. She has made numerous attempts to hook back up with Dudley, but he knows you can't turn a whore into a house wife.

- **Uncle Bernie** has his own bail bonds company, him and Dudley still talks everyday.

THE END

DEDICATION

First I would like to thank God for not giving up on me and blessing me with the gift of living life.

I dedicate my first book to my Daughter Brittany Kierra Thompson for the inspiration of constantly keeping me in the mind frame to use my mind wisely. Time passes by so fast and now you are in college.

Thanks to my mother (Carolyn Watlington) for raising 3 kids, I was a handful to raise. Your hard work, honesty and love motivated me to keep reaching for the stars.

Lastly, I would like to thank God again for telling me daily to never give up on my dreams. I'm still thanking him daily.

A.Dakala